DISCARD

OWEN COUNTY PUBLIC LIBRARY
10 SOUTH MONTGOMERY ST.
SPENCER, IN 47460

THE DOWAGER DUCHESS

THE DOWAGER DUCHESS

•

Joye Ames

AVALON BOOKS
NEW YORK

© Copyright 2002 by Joyce and James Lavene
Library of Congress Catalog Card Number: 2002090085
ISBN 0-8034-9537-4
All rights reserved.
All the characters in this book are fictitious,
and any resemblance to actual persons,
living or dead, is purely coincidental.
Published by Thomas Bouregy & Co., Inc.
160 Madison Avenue, New York, NY 10016

PRINTED IN THE UNITED STATES OF AMERICA
ON ACID-FREE PAPER
BY HADDON CRAFTSMEN, BLOOMSBURG, PENNSYLVANIA

then looked up at her steward and smiled. "Let's continue on."

Will Sheldon, already Her Grace's adoring servant after only two weeks in her employ, blushed to the roots of his carrot red hair. He could see he must strive to become a better horseman. He pushed his spectacles back on his nose then struck out after her, throwing caution to the wind.

Horses had always been his secret fear. Louisa, for that was how he thought of her, would hear the estate details outdoors and on horseback, whenever possible. Thus, he must learn not to be afraid, for her sake. It hadn't taken him that long to realize that he wished she would once look at him like she did that monster horse of hers! Nostradamus was a frightening brute in his opinion. Certainly not a fit mount for a Duchess! But then the Duke was dead and there was no man to tell her nay to anything she decided to do.

Why she hadn't married after the Duke's death five years ago was a major source of speculation at Osbourne Park. She was wealthy, young, beautiful. Certainly desirable! Men wanted her. Suitors were as regular as clockwork around the estate. They were on her like Ulysses' chiefs on Penelope! He believed the men of the aristocracy must not have their wits about them or they would see this wasn't the way to proceed with Louisa.

"Mr. Sheldon?"

Will Sheldon's head bobbed up like an apple in a barrel. He was momentarily taken away by his thoughts. He brought them abruptly back to the woman at his side. "That is all there is for today, Your Grace," he told her in his usual serious manner. He brought his thoughts and his mount up to par.

The two horses walked sedately together along the path

My Dear Louisa;

By all means, feel free to use the town house. Fleet and the staff will be so happy to have you. As you know, Charles was partial to the house. I am happy at the site and now that the war seems to be over, cannot conceive of spending time in London.

Good fortune to you and Elsbeth
L.

Chapter One

Louisa, Duchess of Osbourne, swept her hat from her hair with an easy, careless gesture. The thick, white blond hair was nearly blown free from its confines anyway. It was a glorious day! The sun was warm, the breeze light and teasing on her cheek.

Her horse danced restlessly beneath her and she patted the Arabian's neck. "I know you, Nostradamus," she told him caressingly. "Never enough, is there? You could run on forever." She gazed out over the open, rolling hills, green as emerald, kissed by dew. "I could too, you know. But there is work to do."

Nostradamus snorted and pawed at the ground, letting her know what he thought of the notion.

A gray gelding cantered slowly back to them, its rider less than steady in his saddle. "Is there a problem, Your Grace?"

"No." She patted Nostradamus' glossy mane once more,

Outwitted

He drew a circle that shut me out—
Hectic, rebel, a thing to flout.
But Love and I had wit to win:
We drew a circle that took him in!

—Edwin Markham

between the trees. From there, only the tile roof of Osbourne was visible along the landscape. Two-hundred-year-old oaks surrounded the house like a fortress.

"Oh, never say so, Mr. Sheldon," she replied quickly. "Are we to return to that stuffy house so soon?"

He gulped hard. His eyes were apologetic when they returned to her face. He was not sure what to say. He looked down at the list he'd brought with him. Rents. Repairs. Crops being planted. Drainage. He supposed he *could* make up some matter of business.

Louisa laughed. "I am only teasing you, Mr. Sheldon. I am certain to be late anyway. We leave for London on the morrow. No doubt *something* vital is to be done."

Sheldon cleared his throat and found his voice. "Will you be gone long, Your Grace?"

Louisa frowned. "A difficult question, Mr. Sheldon. I hope not to be gone the entire season but we will have to do what is necessary to find Beth a husband she can tolerate."

That was not news. Everyone in The Park knew they were going and they all knew it was because of bad blood between Her Grace and her brother's wife.

"I understand, Your Grace. A pity the problem could not have been dealt with in a less distracting fashion."

"Ah, but Beth's Mama will have her pound of flesh, Mr. Sheldon. So we had best be up to it. I shall race you back to the house."

Will knew that no power on earth would send him hurtling after his employer. He took his own time with his animal and his thoughts. He shook his head as he watched her skirts flying. The Duchess was an original.

Louisa was too caught up in her own thoughts to pay attention to her young steward's riding habits. He seemed to be a good man of business. Even if he was a trifle serious. She was possessed that morning by thoughts of leaving Osbourne. She had only visited London once in her life. It had been an unqualified disaster. She wished she could avoid it now.

She sighed, knowing she could not. Beth's Mama had insisted on her daughter marrying a Viscount old enough to be her father to help settle her own accounts. The young girl had flown to her aunt's protection rather than marry the lout her mother proposed.

Louisa had promised to give Beth a Season where she would have her pick of titled gentlemen. She wouldn't stand for her brother's only child being abused in that fashion. Her brother, Michael, couldn't be there to protect her. That left Louisa.

She couldn't bear thinking about her brother, she decided, roughly wiping a tear from the corner of her eye. Her brother had been missing since the last battle on the Peninsula. They had yet to find him. Louisa prayed every morning for his safe recovery. She refused to believe that he would not return to them. She listened attentively to every tale about lost brothers and fathers found unexpectedly. But in the meantime, she had to protect her niece!

Everyone at the estate knew they were bound for London for the Season. What they didn't know was that money had changed hands as well to secure her niece's future. Louisa had gladly paid her sister-in-laws' debts to keep her from dragging Beth into a loveless marriage. But she knew Beth's mother. Alice would not be satisfied. The woman went through money like water through a sieve! Louisa knew she must take Beth away from her greedy Mama.

No one would know what leaving the estate cost her personally. Louisa frowned, as the stable yard came into

The Dowager Duchess

view. London was a place she had not thought to see again. She was happy at Osbourne. There was nothing the city could offer her. To think of leaving was nearly more than she could bear. But she had promised Beth, she reflected, bringing an unsatisfied Nostradamus from a heavy gallop down to a sedate trot as they reached the stable. She would not let her brother's child down.

"Lose Mr. Sheldon again, have ye?"

Louisa looked behind her, slipping from Nostradamus' back while Ben held his head. "It would seem so. But he is coming along quite nicely. I expect by the end of the summer, he'll be riding as though born to it."

Ben Roberts grimaced as he watched the stocky, ginger-haired man coming towards them, half on, half off his saddle. "If ye say so, Yer Grace."

"Ben." She lowered her voice so that the others starting to mill around them couldn't hear. "You have known me all my life. Why must you persist in calling me by my title? You have called me names my mother would have blushed to hear before my father died."

She stared at the homely man who had been with her for as long as she could recall. Where he had come from or how old he was, she truly did not know. Ben was enigmatic, sharing only what he had to and keeping the rest behind the mask of his weather-beaten face.

"As I told ye before, *Yer Grace*. I'll give respect where it's due."

The two glared at each other. Ben's wizened squint won, as it always did. There was a scar that ran from his left eye to his hairline that made her think of where he had been and things that he had done. He had a way of using it to his advantage, making it turn white against his brown face, making her squirm. She had tried as an adult to outlast it, but it worked as well as it had when she was twelve.

Louisa turned away from him, glancing to where Mr. Sheldon was attempting to dismount with the aid of a stable hand.

"Although, I'll say ye don't look too proper right now," Ben added and as she turned around quickly, "Yer Grace."

True, the ancient brown riding skirt had seen better days, she considered. Her green jacket was stained with mud from the field they'd walked through while it was being seeded. Her hair was no longer pushed under the sedate brown hat she'd started out with earlier that day.

She often forgot about her appearance when she was riding around the estate. A simple luxury she wouldn't be able to afford in the city and yet another reason her spirit ached not to leave.

She curtsied low to the older man who'd taught her to ride when she could barely walk. "Perhaps you should call me something more suitable then, since I do not meet with your exacting specifications."

Ben spat down into the dirt as she spun away. Too much learnin'. Specifications, indeed! And folks wondered why the chit didn't marry!

"Are you all right, Mr. Sheldon?" Louisa asked, coming to her steward's side as she helped him steady himself on his feet.

"What? Oh, yes. Yes." He pushed his glasses up higher on his nose. His face was nearly as red as his hair.

"I am relying on you while I am gone. I am persuaded that you will do an excellent job."

"Yes, Your Grace." He stumbled as they walked towards the house. She righted him. "Everything will be as it should be. Have no thought about it being otherwise. You can place your trust in me."

"And you will continue your riding lessons," she reminded him, brushing a leaf and twig from his gray jacket.

"Of, of course," he agreed. Her hand on his arm made his stomach shoot up into his throat.

"I trust you implicitly." Louisa smiled up into his politely affable face. "I am going to call you Will when we are alone. Is that agreeable?"

"Yes, Your Grace."

"And you will call me Louisa."

"Of course, Your-er-Louisa." He swallowed hard. He already thought of her in too many, too familiar ways. She was very personable. Far *too* personable.

"Thank you, Will. If you will get those accounts ready for me, I shall be down to sign them later."

"Yes, Your-er-Louisa."

He couldn't understand why she'd picked him to be her secretary but he knew he'd have his throat torn out before he'd make her sorry. He had never had a position of trust quite like this one. Well, he'd never actually *had* a position at all before this one but that was not the point. Her Grace, the Duchess of Osbourne, was very relaxed in her manner. It was no wonder that his predecessor had taken advantage of it. But surely only a scoundrel would take advantage of such a lady! He knew he would never...

Louisa stopped abruptly as they followed the mellowed stone walkway to the sunlit house. Her eyes rested lovingly on the sturdy walls and sloping roof, following the deep bed of red tulips to the curve of the drive.

Mr. Sheldon nearly fell over her. He put out his hands to catch himself and touched her arm. She offered him her hand in assistance. He took it in his own as though it were made of rice paper. She was so delicate, like a flower herself, and yet so competent.

Louisa groaned as she recognized the bright yellow curricle in the drive, a nondescript horse tied to the post in front of it.

"Something wrong, Your Grace?" Will asked, instantly frowning when she looked up at him. "I mean, Louisa."

"I suppose not." She sighed. "You'll have to meet him sooner or later, Will. My cousin, Andrew. He hasn't been here since, well, since I dismissed Mr. Beatty."

Dismissed was a gentle word for that unfortunate occurrence. Will knew the story already. How the Duchess had caught her previous man of business stealing from her tenants. And how he had possessed the temerity to blame a young man from one of the farms for his misdeeds.

When she'd found him whipping the lad, the Duchess had ridden down on him with hellfire in her eyes, or so one of the grooms related the story. She had used her own riding crop on the man, thrashing him twice before he would give up on the boy. Beatty had come after her, snatching the crop from her hand but he had been subdued by Ben Roberts. It was still the talk of the estate three months later.

Louisa, much to her neighbors' and employees' chagrin, had refused to press charges against the man, saying that it was enough to turn him away without reference. Will Sheldon could not agree. He would have insisted that the Duchess hand the man over to the proper authorities. But he wasn't in a position to disagree since he hadn't been there.

He kept his own council and stared at the yellow racing curricle in the drive. The entire family was colorful, to say the least.

"Andrew is rather like Uncle Bertie," Louisa told him

slowly as they resumed their forward pace towards the house.

A relative that lived off the estate, Will translated the information. Another of the hangers-on that the late Duke had left his young daughter. Much the same way as the furniture and the fountain in the garden. The estate was one of the wealthiest in England yet it was entailed in its own way. The Duchess had been left with great responsibilities. Mainly, a family of parasites who continuously plied her for monies.

Several pairs of interested eyes watched them from within the confines of the house, barely pushing aside a rich, velvet hanging to see without being seen.

"She needs to be married, by Gad." Uncle Bertie emphasized the thought by tapping his heavy cane on the floor. The effect was somewhat dampened by the thick Axminster carpet underfoot but not entirely lost on his companion.

"Picked a young 'un this time," Uncle Reggie observed.

Uncle Bertie snorted. "After that Beatty affair, she should have been picking out a husband and having babies."

"What are you two old codgers up to?" A younger man joined them at the window. "Oh. So there she is."

"With her steward. Look at her hair! Looks like Medusa!"

Andrew Drayton, Marquess of Osbourne, considered his cousin's appearance. She was slender but almost too tall. She moved gracefully and had a well-turned ankle. Her pale hair reminded him of champagne, a rare shade. The color of moonlight. There was a hint of roses in her lips and cheeks from the fast ride home and her eyes were a misty blue. A face and form to write sonnets about! A sweet voice and a fortune to boot! What man could want more?

But she was a cold, hard woman. He knew that from experience. Watching her come towards him might have aroused him had he been another man, and she, another woman. The sight of her made him shudder at the battle that was to come. But if she had thought to see him beg for the money that was rightfully his, she was going to be disappointed!

Another man sat at his ease in a corner of the room and watched them all, listening to their words. The Marquess hadn't noticed him, as he'd come slamming into the house a few moments before. The uncles had been too intent on their feminine prey. So, Devon, Lord Stanton, waited where the butler had left him, without making his presence known. It was a new experience for him to be ignored. Usually, he was a man of notice.

The butler had looked at him with disdain as well. Another unusual occurrence. He would have to remember to have his valet cast his clothing into the fire. Obviously, he was not dressed as well as he had thought that morning. To be looked down on by a country butler and ignored by three hayseeds was too much, indeed, for his vanity!

Lord Stanton heard a commotion at the front door and watched as the three other men in the room took their places as though they hadn't noticed the mistress' approach. An interesting household.

"Good afternoon, Your Grace." Gervis greeted her at the door, taking her dirty jacket and gloves in one hand, her hat in the other.

"It was." She sighed at her reflection in the gilded mirror behind the large bouquet of daffodils. She could be thankful it was only Andrew. She looked like a gypsy with her hair blown so wildly and no time to repair it before the battle her cousin represented. "Where is he?"

"In the front parlor, Your Grace. Shall I have refreshments served?" Gervis only glanced once at her less than dignified appearance but his eyes spoke volumes. He had never approved of the Duchess, despite the fact that he respected her abilities to run the estate. Even that was a dual-edged regard since he did not believe that a woman should do more than be decorative. He had expressed his opinion more than once to the cook and the housekeeper.

"Yes, please, Gervis." She was looking at Will but she still felt the butler's disapproving visage. She had learned to disregard it. "You might as well join us. It won't be pleasant but you need to get adjusted. Andrew still has a few months until he reaches his majority."

All three men had moved away from the window by the time the door opened. Uncle Bertie sat at his usual spot across from Uncle Reggie, draughts between them. Neither looked up at her entrance. It was always the same.

"Good afternoon, Andrew." Louisa spoke first, determined to try to be civil, though she knew well enough what lay ahead.

"Good afternoon?" Andrew laughed, pacing the floor. "Is *that* what you call it?"

Louisa drew a deep breath and glanced at Will Sheldon before she faced her cousin. "All right, Andrew. What is it this time?"

"You know bloody well what it is, Louisa!"

A collective gasp went up from the uncles who were supposedly engrossed in their game. Their eyes, however, never left the board.

"About the debts—"

"About the debts," he agreed. "Those are a Gentleman's Debts of Honor. You cannot refuse to pay them!"

"Until you are five and twenty and in possession of the

title and your portion of the estate, I can and will refuse any and all debts that are extravagant and extreme."

He glared at her. "What is it you want me to do with my time while I wait to reach my majority, Cousin? Stay in the house and read? Or perhaps learn to sew? Would that suit your purpose?"

"I have no purpose, Andrew. Except to keep you from making an even bigger fool of yourself than you have already!"

The two faced each other defiantly across the room. Their words were rapiers, attempting to draw blood. Another gasp went up. Will shifted uneasily.

Gervis served tea during the silence that followed in the pleasant room with its sky-blue draperies and deeper blue carpets and furniture. It was a room for light conversation and easy companionship. A room the late Duke had loved for its sense of peace, particularly during his long illness.

"Sit down, Andrew," Louisa requested. Gervis set the tea set before her on the rosewood table. "Perhaps we can find a course of action that will suit both of us."

She watched him. His thoughts flickered across his handsome young face. He possessed the Osbourne looks and temper in abundance. She always faced him calmly, despite his tantrums. He was dressed in the height of fashion, as always. His boots caught the light, polished to almost a mirror finish. The cut and cloth of his breeches and coat were excellent. She knew they cost a pretty penny since she was the one to pay the bootmaker's bill for them.

"I cannot believe a relative of mine so imbecilic as to put a woman in charge of the family's fortune." His voice was low and angry. "I want you to know I have appealed to Uncle Forrest for help."

"That's fine, Andrew. Though I cannot imagine what good you think that will do."

His shoulders were straight beneath the dark coat. He squared his chin. "I knew it would be a waste of time to appeal to you personally. You never understand."

"Not quite," Louisa said, seating herself at the table. She poured a cup of tea for herself and Will Sheldon into fine Sevres china. "I shall pay these last debts. I was hoping you would come to visit since I have a proposition for you."

"What do you mean?" he demanded, his gray eyes hard but hopeful.

"I mean that I intend to increase your allowance, Andrew. Perhaps I should have done so earlier. However—" She looked up at him. He kept himself from flinching at the ice in her eyes only by practice. "I will not countenance any more gaming for high stakes. I do not care one whit if you have to leave the country until you come of age. Send me another debt for that much and I will turn it back to you. I hope you understand?"

"Certainly, Cousin." He was relieved but would not have shown her that emotion if it had meant his entire fortune. "I must say that I am pleasantly surprised by your change of heart."

Despite himself, Andrew had to admit that the room was a perfect foil for her. She was like a rare jewel set in its case. Beautiful and untouchable. He was certain he could have been quite besotted if she had not been the most vile witch he had ever chanced to encounter.

"You are less than a year away from managing your own accounts," she reminded him sensibly. "If you can learn now to manage them wisely, you can add to your fortune rather than lose everything."

He nodded, barely interested in her sage advice. "Thank you, Louisa. I will attempt to be wise."

"Will you stay for tea?" she asked quietly.

"No, thank you. I have other, more pressing business, in the city."

"As you will," she acknowledged, refusing to notice that her hands trembled ever so slightly. The other pairs of eyes were not so blind.

The door closed quietly behind Andrew. A crystal vase of pink roses shook slightly in the draft that he created. Louisa dared to take a deep breath. Her shoulders sagged a little in relief.

"An unpleasant young man." Uncle Bertie spoke suddenly into the silence that followed.

"In my day," Uncle Reggie began, reaching for his tea and cake, "one would not have spoken to any relation in that manner. Even though the circumstances are . . . unfortunate."

It was at that moment that Louisa noticed the man in the corner near the door. He was getting to his feet as she started to her own. His gaze caught hers and didn't move away.

"Oh dear," she began, feeling a hot blush come up on her cheeks. "I am afraid we have aired our dirty linen in public. You must be Lord Stanton?"

"I suppose I must," he agreed with a smile tracing its way across his lips as he moved towards her. "Your Grace."

She looked down at the back of his head as he touched his lips to her hand. Instinct told her to snatch that member back as she felt his touch. Instead she could only marvel at the way the sun had kissed his otherwise dark hair, golden streaks highlighting the thick strands. When he lifted his head, she looked into his eyes. They were hazel,

The Dowager Duchess 15

slightly more green than brown, fringed by incredibly long black lashes. His face was striking but also showed signs of humor with its wide smile and the tiny lines that fanned out from his eyes.

"It has been a very long time," she managed.

"Since we were children," he agreed. "May I say how kind the years have been to you?"

Louisa looked away uncomfortably. "I hope you will accept my apology, my lord. I had no idea that you were there." She was suddenly unsure where to place her gaze. Her eyes found his lean, tanned fingers. There was a distinctive signet ring on his left hand. She recognized it as his family crest.

"No apology needed, Your Grace. It was unfortunate, but I can assure you that I was napping the entire occasion and heard nothing. It is I who most apologize for not attending the conversation. The fatigue from the long ride, you know."

It was a polite reply but then, she expected no less. Of course, he had heard it all, but there was little to be done about it. She glanced up into his expressive face and caught the edge of laughter lurking there.

Will Sheldon came up, deliberately obtrusive beside them.

"My steward, Mr. Sheldon," she introduced the two men. Uncle Bertie cleared his throat and Louisa smiled. "Lord Stanton; my uncles. Uncle Bertie, Uncle Reggie, Lord Stanton. He is here to pick up a few of Father's books for a collection of books for the poor."

"You look familiar." Uncle Bertie appraised Lord Stanton's face, his fingers restlessly plucking at the gray tweed of his jacket. "But it's been too long."

Devon smiled in good humor. "It is always surprising

how many people tell one that," he replied calmly. "Just yesterday, a woman told me how very much I resemble the Prince."

They laughed at that and the moment passed. Uncle Reggie claimed Uncle Bertie's attention on the game again. He had already forgotten that they were supposed to be listening to the conversation and was involved with winning.

"Would you care for tea, my lord?" Louisa asked, feeling drab in her suddenly rustic skirt and white silk blouse that had seen a few too many washings. Now she wished she had taken the time to change and freshen up after her ride. She no doubt smelled of horses and wet dirt.

His gaze went over her lightly but was disconcertingly thorough. "Nothing would please me more, Your Grace. However, I am sadly late for another appointment. I did not know if you would be at home for me to speak to. If we could—"

"Of course!" She moved around from the table. "I must apologize for keeping you waiting as well. The day was so unusually clear, I'm afraid I lost myself in it."

She smiled up into his face and he found himself unable to look away for just an instant. Her eyes were as astonishingly clear as the day she had just described. Her lovely face was turned up to him. Without thought, he took a step closer to her.

Will Sheldon eyed the engrossed couple narrowly. While he had not liked the younger nephew, there was something he disliked even more about this man. Hadn't everyone warned him about men hunting the duchess? This man may have come through the front door instead of the kitchen, as one suitor had last week, but he looked no less predatory. He made to stand and accompany them to the library.

"Do not trouble yourself, Will." She put a hand on his

arm. "Finish your tea and attend to those papers. I can find the books for Lord Stanton."

Her steward was unhappy with the concept but he bowed his head. "Of course, Your Grace."

"Thank you. My lord, if you will come this way?"

"I have brought a list of books that the late Duke promised to us." Devon offered her the paper with the Duke's seal on it. "If these books are too difficult for you, I would gladly take whatever is available."

"I'm certain it won't be too difficult." Louisa took the paper from his hand gingerly, leading the way through the door. "It will only take a moment."

She led him down the hall towards the library while Gervis and Will Sheldon looked on after them.

"You know, I believe I could find my way through here blindfolded," Devon quipped. "I remember this house so well from my youth."

"My parents did love to have guests when I was a child," Louisa recalled. "My father and yours remained great friends to the end of their lives."

"Yes," he agreed. "My father was terribly distressed to hear of your father's passing."

"I had heard that you had returned from the war."

"Finally!" He pushed open the heavy oak door for her. "I feel I've been gone an age."

"At least you came home," she said with a small smile. "Michael is missing, I fear."

"Michael? I had no idea! Where was he last seen?"

"The last campaign on the Peninsula. I've had people looking for him but as yet, there is no news."

"How terrible for you," he replied. "If I can be of service, please don't hesitate to call on me."

"Thank you, my lord. You know, I barely remember you. You went off to school when I was quite young."

"I recall you being very short. Your hair was in braids and you had jam on your face," he responded with a laugh. "You've grown—quite well."

"Thank you, my lord," she demurred. "Shall we find those books?"

Chapter Two

Andrew stalked out of the house, snatching his hat from Gervis as he went. There was just no dealing with the woman! She could easily have released all of his funds to him. He was the heir to Osbourne, after all! She could only dole out his estate to him for so long!

Unfortunately, there was no one else to appeal to on his behalf. His own father was dead and Uncle Forrest had turned his head when he'd spoken to him. In the time since the death of his uncle, the Duke, he had connived with many of his friends and family to speak for him. It had not made any difference in Louisa's attitude. And usually, they came away respecting her and taking her side on the matter!

One could look anywhere on the sprawling estate and see the brilliant work she'd done in the past four years. It was apparent even to him and he hated the harridan! It was unnatural! She thought she could handle a man's responsibilities! She should have married and had children and been living on her own estate instead of worrying about his!

It was only a few months to his majority, but they would be long months. Even then, he would get his share of the money but only the small dower house on the estate. Unless Louisa married or chose to leave her residence, he would never truly have his inheritance. It was galling! A Duke without an estate!

Louisa had already let him take possession of the townhouse in London but only because she chose never to be there. She'd given over the hunting lodge in Scotland but he didn't choose to be there. Obviously these concessions represented some gap in her method of torture.

What were the chances that the woman would marry? he asked himself. She had turned down offers from some of the most eligible bachelors in England. She had made it clear that she had no intention of marrying. And why should she? She had a grand estate and servants and could come and go as she saw fit. Her coffers were full and there was no one to peek over her shoulder and ask how she spent her money!

The only other way would be if she died. That was probably the *only* way she would lose both the estate and the inheritance. But what were the chances of that? She looked positively hale and hearty and she would only be twenty and three on her next birthday!

He crammed his jaunty traveling hat down on his head. He could only hope Cousin Louisa married again, which seemed unlikely. Or that she lived a very short life. Which seemed just as unlikely. He would, no doubt, live all of his life in her shadow. He would have the title but everything else of importance would belong to her.

Andrew stepped out the door into the sunlight and suddenly thoughts of dying seemed appropriate as the world turned upside down. He found himself lying on his back, halfway down the stairs. A large hairy form was standing squarely on his chest, drooling into his face.

"Get down, Brutus, there's a good boy," someone called soothingly.

"*Good boy?*" Andrew gasped, trying to get out from under the beast. "Good boy? He nearly killed me."

The hairy beast's wet doggy form was replaced by a sweet young face with sympathetic blue eyes, the color of a summer sky. Her hair was golden light framing a countenance that made the Marquess certain that he had indeed died and was beginning to see angels.

"I am so sorry! He does get away from me. Can I help you up?"

He waved away her hand, tiny and clean in its white glove. He was suddenly feeling much stronger and was on his feet in a snap. "I'm fine. Only a little dirty from the beast's paws." He brushed at his yellow breeches while he peeped surreptitiously at the trim, feminine form in the pale green gown.

"Perhaps you should go inside and have Gervis clean those for you before they stain," she suggested pleasantly, taking a dainty step back.

"Perhaps," he found himself agreeing. He let The Vision of Beauty take his arm and lead him back into the house he had fled from only moments before.

"Brutus is only a puppy," she explained, "and as such is a trifle free-spirited. Do you know anything about training dogs?"

He looked down into her pretty, querying face and was divested of any thought except how sweet it might be to kiss those soft pink lips. "Dog-er-training?"

"Yes. Aunt Louisa says I must send him away to be trained but I had been hoping to find someone who could do it here. I should like to watch, in case there are any problems in the future."

"Aunt Louisa?" he asked, hearing the hated name through a cloud of soft white gauze. Who was this enchanting creature? He suddenly realized what she'd said. "*Aunt Louisa?*"

"Yes. Oh, I am so sorry. I am Miss Elsbeth Montgomery." Her hands flew to her mouth. "Oh no! That is wrong as well. I do not believe I am supposed to introduce myself. Please forgive me. I have no polish at all, I'm afraid."

"We are family, in a manner of speaking," he assured her, placing her hand back on his arm as they walked up the steps to the house. "I am the Duchess's cousin, the Duke's heir. Which no doubt makes us some family as well."

"Oh!" She smiled, her eyes sparkling. "The Infamous Marquess. Of course! How fabulous to meet you. Is that your curricle?"

What a charming child, he considered, escorting her into the house past Gervis' startled gaze. It was hard to conceive that her aunt should be the witch, Louisa, although he could credit that their eyes were nearly the same color. He deduced that she must be Louisa's missing brother's child.

"Perhaps I can clean up and then we might go for a drive in my curricle?" he suggested, rewarded by a smile that beamed from her dimples to her eyes.

"That would be the best of anything! I'll have Brutus tied out while I wait."

He left her in the hall, hurrying up the stairs to find assistance cleaning his coat. He looked back once, amply pleased to see her looking back at him. She blushed delightfully and hurried away. He looked around himself at the top of the stairs, giving a passing inspection of all the ancient relatives' paintings in heavy frames. Perhaps good was to be found in the most unlikely places.

Devon remembered the Duke as being a kind man, hard working and well thought of by his peers. While never inspired to be more than a country squire, he loved his home and his family. It was hard to imagine him being so unorthodox as to leave his estate to his daughter. He had heard a rumor that her brother had chosen not to take the title, a rare enough happening. He wondered what would happen to her when Andrew took over the estate.

Devon determined that he would hear the whole story before it was over. Of course, meeting Louisa again was a tale in itself. She was charming, beautiful, intelligent, and clearly, her own mistress. Was that why the Duke had trusted her with the estate until his heir came of age?

"How is the charity faring?" Louisa asked him as they entered the room. "I heard you had taken over from your father after your return from France."

"It has raised a considerable amount," Devon told her. "My father's dream of teaching the poor to read has acquired some noble aid. The Prince himself has promised some of his personal library."

Louisa laughed. "Ah! The Regent should bring you some important names! Perhaps you could convince my cousin of the importance of giving as well as getting."

"Your Grace—"

"It is all right. I know you couldn't help being there. Just as Andrew could not help being himself."

Devon looked away, not replying. Obviously, the young pup had been encouraged to say whatever he felt to his cousin. Even the uncles had not spoken up in her defense. He knew the late Duke would have given the boy the thrashing of his life for such impertinence.

He had noticed the remarkable beauty and order of the estate when he had driven in that morning. The Duke had known what he was doing, leaving Louisa in charge. The estate was well cared for by an extraordinary woman with eyes the color of the Mediterranean. A woman that he intended to know much better in the very near future. Now that he had made her acquaintance again after so many years, he wouldn't be so negligent of her in the future.

"It should be quite simple to find these books," Louisa was saying, staring up at the book-lined walls. "However, they aren't on the bottom shelves." She began to climb the ladder.

"Allow me, Your Grace," Devon said at once, going to take her place on the first wooden rung. "I should be pleased to do the climbing."

Their fingers touched briefly on the smooth wooden rail as they passed. Louisa moved quickly, as though scalded. She held her hand to her chest. "It comes from being alone and dependent on one's self," she replied with a laugh, steadying the ladder for him. "It has been a very revealing process since my father died."

Devon did some quick mental calculations, guessing at her age when the Duke had died. "It must have been a strain for you, inheriting the management of so vast an estate. You are very young to carry that burden."

"Not so young as I was when it happened," she reminded him as he reached for a book. "It was quite devastating at the time. But now that I have it under control, I would not have it any other way."

"Freedom is a heady drought," he agreed, catching a

glimpse of the smooth white curve of her breast as she pressed against the ladder. He forced himself to look away. He was, after all, he reminded himself sternly, a gentleman in most situations.

"I see you read Wordsworth," he said, looking at the copy of *Intimations of Immortality*. "Have you seen *The Excursion* as yet?"

"No," she replied, "but I shall as quickly as I can find a copy. I have heard they were forced to print another edition despite what Lord Francis Jeffrey said about it."

"He is one of the few critics," Devon continued. "Lamb and Keats both feel it is brilliant."

"But they are his contemporaries," she enjoined, reaching for the book he dropped down to her. "One would expect them to support him."

"I don't believe Keats is so easily persuaded against his own best interests," he answered. "If the book was not worthy, he would consider it his duty to tell the world just to save his own hide."

Louisa laughed. "Is he really so self serving?"

He glanced down at her. The sound of her laughter was like music. "You should come to London and find out."

She frowned and turned her head away. "I'm sure it wouldn't be worth that effort to find out, my lord."

"There are other—persons of interest—in London who would be glad to make your stay worth the effort," he encouraged her.

Only an instant later, something large and wet bounded into the room, knocking the ladder askew. Louisa had a brief feeling of falling backward as the ladder pushed by her. She sat down hard on the carpet. A book landed in her lap. Beth's dog dodged the debris of falling books and ran from the room.

Louisa traced the line of wreckage from the fleeing dog to the ladder then to the man who lay on the floor, his head very near her feet.

"Lord Stanton!" She got to her knees and crawled to him, looking down into his pale face. His eyes were closed and he was very still. Louisa laid her head on his chest, praying for a muffled heartbeat. When she heard it, she pushed up enough to lean over him, loosening his intricate neck cloth. "Lord Stanton?" she called again softly. "Can you hear me?"

He groaned in answer and moved slightly, shifting his position on the hard floor. His arms slowly came up around her, bringing her close against him. He didn't attempt to hold her there. His arms just rested loosely against her.

Chest to chest, her lips formed a soft, "*Oh!*"

He opened his eyes and looked at her but didn't speak.

"Lord Stanton?" She addressed him when she saw his eyes flutter open.

She tried to impel her body into movement but nothing happened. Alarm bells jangled in her head but their din was fuzzy at best. His warmth seemed to soak into her, making her feel languid and weak.

"Oh my! Aunt Louisa! I shall go get Gervis!" Beth took in the situation and raced into the room then back out again.

"Are you all right, my lord?" Louisa queried.

"I could not be more so," he replied a trifle breathlessly.

"I am sorry. I've known that creature was a hazard but I hated to make her give it up."

"If I may?" he inquired briefly.

She nodded and his hands encircled her waist, helping her to her feet. He stood up beside her. She caught him, her arms going around his chest, as he swayed a little.

"Your Grace?" he inquired, not realizing that he wasn't sound.

"I am so sorry, Lord Stanton. I know it sounds improper but if you could perhaps hold still just there for a moment, I think I shall be able to help you until someone comes."

As it was not in his nature to rebuke the tender trap her arms made around him, his own arms came to rest loosely about her again. Her waist was small and supple. Her body had been indescribably arousing pressed against his on the floor. She smelled of fresh air and some floral scent he couldn't quite identify.

"I am afraid it has become impossible for me to know if the fall has injured me," he told her quietly.

Louisa stood with her head against his chest, hearing the slow steady beat of his heart in her ear. His hands were warm and gentle on her back. His body leaned heavily towards her. *Where was Gervis?* "It will be all right, my lord," she replied calmly. "You have just had a knock on the head."

"I am afraid it is more, Your Grace," he answered so quietly that she had to move slightly so that she could see his face. "I am quite dizzy and not at all lucid."

She wanted to call out for Gervis to hurry but she lost the thought as she looked into his green eyes. He was so handsome, with his arrogant cheekbones and his chiseled lips.

Slowly, something welled up inside of her that was more than dizzying. A surge of awareness so powerful it nearly folded her knees beneath her. She felt her face become warm. Her heart doubled its normal beat. "I am sorry," she whispered yet again, not realizing how very close his face was to her own.

Devon felt the pull of her in every pore of his body. He

recognized it for what it was: *desire*. Her pale hair spilled silkily over his arm as he drew her closer to him. He could see the amazement in her light blue eyes as they widened to encompass his face. That she felt as he did was written clearly on her fine features. That it surprised her was even more obvious.

"Lord Stanton," she whispered, her lips moving closer to his. "I wouldn't like to see you injured any further."

"Madame." He stroked a gentle hand through her hair. "I'll willingly take my chances."

Devon knew he would always wonder afterward what that kiss would have tasted like, but at that moment the door swung wide again. The room filled with servants. The young woman who'd loosed the beast on them in the first place was crying and wringing her hands. The moment had passed, never to come again.

Pushing aside the butler's suggestion that a burly footman should carry him to a chamber, Devon asked for a glass of brandy and a chair. Louisa nodded as Gervis looked to her for a decision.

"It might be a good idea to send for a doctor," she suggested in a squeaky voice she didn't recognize as her own. She urged herself to calm down and to think straight. Lord Stanton could be seriously injured and all *she* could consider was how close he had come to kissing her.

Two footmen guided the injured man to a chair. Just as they reached it, Lord Stanton's knees gave way. His face was very pale and his eyes were closed. The large footman, Tom, caught him and lifted him easily. He looked at the Duchess for further instruction.

"Take him up to the guest room next to mine, please, Tom," Louisa said briskly, sending the other footman for the doctor.

"Is that wise, Your Grace?" Will Sheldon asked as they followed the footman up the stairs.

"Wise, Mr. Sheldon?" she inquired, running forward to open the door to the chamber.

"I mean, we know nothing about him. To put him so near your own room—"

"I quite agree with Mr. Sheldon," Gervis added.

Louisa gave them both an impatient glance. "It will be fine, Mr. Sheldon. Do not worry, Gervis. I shall handle it from here."

"What the devil is going on up here?" Uncle Bertie demanded, hobbling up the stairs.

"Lord Stanton was hurled from the ladder when Miss Elsbeth's dog ran through the library," Mr. Sheldon told him.

"Eh?" Uncle Reggie queried. "Who was thrown from a ladder?"

"Will he be all right, Aunt Louisa?" Beth wondered. "I shall never forgive myself if—"

"Don't worry. Lord Stanton will be fine," her aunt reassured her.

Will Sheldon didn't move from his place beside the bed where Tom the footman had put Lord Stanton. Even though the other man was lying silently, with his eyes closed, Will didn't trust him.

"I'll fetch some cool cloths and your maid," Gervis said, leaving the room with a glance that brought Tom with him out the door.

Louisa looked at Mr. Sheldon. "You see. He is quite harmless. If you would see to Elsbeth, I shall tend Lord Stanton. Please bring the doctor up when he comes."

Will watched as Louisa bent over her patient. He started to protest but held his tongue. He had worked with the aristocracy long enough to know the Voice of Authority. As usual, the Duchess was slightly eccentric in her attitude. But Will pushed back his glasses and took Elsbeth's arm.

"Please take Uncle Bertie and Uncle Reggie downstairs too," Louisa suggested. "They both look as though they could do with a drop of brandy after the shock."

"Quite so," Uncle Reggie agreed, nudging Uncle Bertie.

When they had all gone, Louisa took a deep breath and pushed back her sleeves. She had tended her father during his long illness and didn't see a great difference in tending Lord Stanton. She was not a young miss, like Beth, easily influenced by the sight of a man partially dressed.

She removed Lord Stanton's pristine white neck cloth and loosened his shirt. She concentrated on the task and told herself that she would not notice the warm male beneath her kindly ministrations. She wouldn't notice his broad chest or the pulse beating in his throat. She *refused* to notice the way a lock of his hair fell into his face, as he lay there, helpless under her touch. When she had finished, she took a deep, unsteady breath and dared a look at his handsome face. She was taken aback to find his eyes open, his gaze focused on her.

"Are you all right, my lord?" she ventured.

"Since we have come this far, Your Grace," he told her quietly as he pushed himself upright on the pillows behind him, "I believe you should call me Devon."

"You could have broken bones," she told him, pressing him gently back against the bed. "It might be best if you don't move."

"And what of you?" he wondered. "You must have received quite a blow. I was holding several books, as I recall." His fingers touched a spot near her hairline, stroking down her cheek.

The Dowager Duchess 31

She jolted upright away from him, startled at his gesture. "You are indeed quite a handful, my lord," she responded tartly. "But I am unharmed."

"I am fortunate that you were there, or I might not have had help so quickly."

"I should have had Beth send that dog away for training long ago," she answered. "I do apologize."

She felt so odd. Was it possible something *was* wrong with her? It was difficult to draw a complete breath and her head was clouded. Self consciously, she reached to smooth a wrinkle from the pillow near his head. She wished the doctor would come.

"Is there something I can get for you?" She could feel that her smile was tremulous. She didn't move as his thumb brushed her lips. She could almost suppose it happened on accident. She tingled at his warmth.

Devon watched her mouth part softly at his touch. He took a quick breath. A swift flash of desire raced through his bloodstream to his head.

The butler, the maid, and Her Grace's steward convened on the room at once, followed by Andrew and the young woman with the dog. In the chaos of apologies and the arrival of the doctor, there was no time for what might have followed. The doctor, good man that he was, shooed the crowd from the room to examine his patient.

The interview was short and cheerful. Nothing more than a bang on the head. A few days' rest and he would be as good as new. "Of course, you young bucks never listen," the doctor apprised him, putting away his instruments. "Always a girl to chase or a race to win."

"I assure you, Doctor, that I will not be doing any racing or chasing for at least an hour or two," Devon replied.

"You could risk brain fever if you do," the physician

warned, closing his bag. "Should spend the rest of the day in bed at least. Good luck to you."

Devon lay alone in the bedroom, staring at the ceiling. The room, like all other aspects of Osbourne Park, was well cared for and richly appointed. The furniture was heavy and dark but it gleamed with polish and smelled of beeswax. The linen on the bed that surrounded him was clean and recently aired. His mind came full circle to the woman who was responsible for the huge old manor house and the estate.

He felt a deep hunger that refused to stand aside when his mind demanded it let his thoughts pass. His headache was as nothing compared to the ache in another part of him at the thought of the lush fall of Louisa's pale hair and the sweetness of her mouth.

Interested, he considered his own reactions to her. It was unusual for him to be so aware of a woman on such short acquaintance. He was positively overcome! Even without the knock on the head, he might have fallen at her feet. The reaction was nothing less than Cupid-like, the arrow zinging through his head instead of his chest! It was painful and exhilarating.

When the doctor left, the maid came in to inquire if there was anything he needed. He could have answered but that would have sent the poor woman from the room in histrionics!

After his report to Her Grace, the doctor went his way. Will Sheldon attempted to hold the Duchess' thoughts as they made plans for the time she would be gone to London but to no avail. Even as Louisa put her signature to the papers Will put before her, her mind was upstairs in the chamber with Lord Stanton.

Devon. Louisa's mouth curved into a slight smile that

she quickly hid. She wanted to go back and check on him but common sense told her to stay away. There were problems enough in her near future. The next day she would be leaving for London to give Beth her Season. She would leave the staff in charge of the estate. They would have orders to aid Lord Stanton in every way possible until his recovery.

As curious as she was about the strange new feelings Devon had aroused within her, she knew that it was not the time to follow them, *if* there could ever *be* such a time. Danger lay that way. Beth's future had to come first. And then there were her own commitments to consider. She had been alone for a long time. She wasn't sure if she wanted a man in her life. She was happy with the estate and her horses and her friends. Romance, if that was what it was that was making her light-headed and giddy, was probably vastly overrated.

Early the following morning, barely after sunrise, the Duchess and her party left Osbourne Park. She realized that she had been shushing everyone, trying not to awaken Lord Stanton.

There was a part of her that would have liked to stay and discover the promise that he held in his eyes. But the larger part of her was terrified. Her plans were set, she reminded herself. She had thought again and again about her return to London. She had prayed that her sister-in-law would see reason. It hadn't happened. There was only one thing left to do. She had to see her niece through the Season.

Unfortunately, Lord Stanton could have no part in that plan. In fact, he could destroy her niece's chances for happiness if he knew of it. It was for the best, she told herself as she glanced up at the window while the coach started away. She didn't really need a man in her life.

Later that morning, Devon awakened, stiff and sore but feeling quite well rested. He was excited by the prospect of seeing Louisa again. It was surprising to see that light in his eyes as he shaved and dressed, whistling a tune even as he crawled back into his worn clothing. He brushed his dark hair and rubbed at the knot on his head. Nothing could take away from the energy of that morning.

Except to discover that the Duchess was long since gone. She left him a note. He was too vexed at first to read it. The tiny missive, violet colored and scented, sat at his place at the table while her servants brought him breakfast and slipped away from the room.

She had left him. Without a word or even a sigh. He felt like some silly schoolboy who had been put in his place by an entrancing older woman. His instincts were too good to imagine that she had not found him as attractive as he had found her. He had felt her daunting resistance to the idea when they had been close after the accident. But to leave him flat out? That was too much?

He fingered the note curiously, after he sipped at his tea. What had she said to him? Surely, she had not found the entire thing amusing? Or worse, pitied him? He sipped at his tea again then opened the note.

My Lord Stanton,

I am sorry to have to leave you but my plans could not be postponed. My servants will look after you. Please consider my home your own while you recover.

I remain, faithfully,

Louisa Drayton

He read the note over again. It was amazing to him. She

had not so much as *hinted* that there was anything between them. No flirtatious postscript not to try to find her. Not a clue as to where she had gone. It was the most remarkable note he had ever received from a woman.

Was she truly not interested in him? He considered her response to him in the bedroom after the accident. No, he hadn't misread her. He did not believe that was true. He held the scented note up to his nose and closed his eyes, thinking about her beautiful eyes. He would have to find her.

"My Lord?" The dour-faced steward brought him back. "Yes?"

"I was wondering if you had need of the doctor's services again? I could send for him."

"No, that's quite all right," Devon replied, thoughtfully studying the young man. How best to get information from him? He was obviously protective towards his mistress. "Her Grace tells me that she is taking the dog to training."

Will stared at him. "It is not my job to question Her Grace's decisions."

"But this was planned for some while," Devon stated, as though he knew the truth.

"It was," Will replied stiffly. "If that is all?"

Devon nodded. "When we meet in London, I will tell Her Grace how well I was cared for."

The young man flushed. "You are too kind, my lord. I serve Her Grace to the best of my ability."

So, Devon contemplated. Louisa *was* going to London. It surprised him. She was known to be reclusive. In the four years since the Duke had died, she had never partaken of any of the excitements in town. Friends he had spoken to about her weren't really sure what she looked like. She didn't mingle with the *ton* at all.

From the housekeeper, he was able to get more of the story. Miss Elsbeth, the Duchess' niece, was going to town for the Season to find a husband. The Duchess was only going to that den of iniquity to save the poor lamb from some disastrous, arranged marriage. Nothing less would have made the poor Duchess travel to London.

It wouldn't be hard to find Louisa in London, Devon realized, not content simply to give up on her. He had, in fact, been going there himself after a brief stop at his estate. Finding her direction would be simple. He would attend the parties she attended, become friends with the people who befriended her. He would even counsel her as to who would be a good husband for her niece. He would be the pillar she could count on for support while she was marooned in that soulless place.

And he would find what it was that so intrigued him about Louisa Drayton. And why she had avoided contact with him again after their obvious mutual attraction. There was something there between them but it had not been enough to override the sense of fear he felt in her. It was a mystery why she would fight their mutual attraction. And Devon loved a mystery!

Chapter Three

Devon arrived downstairs ready to leave Osbourne, in time to meet Andrew storming out of the house.

"If you're here to see Miss Montgomery, you're too late," the young man warned him.

"I am taking my leave," drawled Devon, glancing at him. "But thank you for your timely advice."

Andrew glanced at him. "I know you, don't I? You're Stanton."

Devon took the reins of the team from his tiger and climbed up on his rig. "Fortunately, we have never been properly introduced."

Andrew's face lightened. "You *are* Stanton, aren't you? I was with your cousin at Eton."

Devon shrugged. "That could be said for a multitude."

The young man's face beamed. "Wait! I saw you here yesterday. You were here aspiring to court my infamous

Cousin Louisa, weren't you?" He laughed out loud. "She attracts them all."

"I don't think you and I need discuss why I was here. Suffice it to say, I witnessed your theatricals yesterday." Could he politely shake this young upstart a little so that his teeth rattled but there was no serious damage?

"The uncles are here but Louisa has removed herself to London for the Season," Andrew filled in what Devon had already ferreted out. "It seems she means to find Miss Montgomery a husband, if the uncles are correct."

"Then I can see my time is wasted here." He saw no reason to illuminate Andrew about anything else that had happened.

"What about Louisa?" Andrew all but rubbed his hands together in anticipation. His eyes roamed the excellent horses and rig enviously. "You mean to marry her, I hope? Ruining her would not do." He had heard of Lord Stanton's exploits before and during the war. If anyone could handle his cousin, it would be Stanton! He stopped short of offering his help since the man was obviously in a foul mood.

Devon drew in a deep breath and his smile was dazzling. "Don't fret, Andrew. I wouldn't have her cut your allowance again."

"What do you mean?" Andrew demanded from the ground.

"Think about it."

Andrew watched Devon's retreating back as his chestnuts began to eat up the road. Fine for him to say, he considered. Stanton Hall had always been his. The money and the famous gardens. He had always had it all. Stanton's parents had died young. No nagging Mama. He was the hero and the golden child. Even his cousin had been Stanton this and Stanton that.

The fact that the other man was on his cousin's scent should have made him happy. He'd heard nothing about Stanton setting up his nursery and it was unlikely he would be looking at Louisa for that task. She was a bit long in the tooth for that! But if he persuaded her to ruin, that might be as good. Even Uncle Forrest might step in to challenge her stranglehold on his money if she began to act out of character.

He didn't feel the least bit of conscience about it either, he told himself as he climbed aboard his curricle. If she hadn't been so hateful to him, he might feel some remorse for her. As it was, the sooner she lost control of Osbourne Park, the better!

The one thing Andrew had really looked forward to, after the hysterics of the previous day, was a ride with Miss Montgomery. It seemed he was to be denied even that. It was too much to bear! He decided he would go to his cousin, Lord Halwell, who lived close by, but on the way he would stop at the Dandy Dunker and get thoroughly drunk.

Devon spent the long ride to town considering his options, weighing his campaign for the lovely Duchess. He savored how he would touch her and what they would say to one another. He smiled when he thought of the wonderful simplicities of life at home. That his one worry should be about a beautiful woman! After the long years of war, it was a welcome relief.

The warm morning sunshine was pleasant on his face. His horses were every bit as spirited as he'd believed they would be when he'd bought them. It had been quite a challenge to have them brought with him first from Spain and then from France. The risk of injury was always present but with careful supervision, he'd brought them back to England safely. It was the same way he'd managed to reach home safely himself.

Now the Bourbon King, however unpopular, would be taking the Little Corporal's place as Monarch of the French. They would all be free again to enjoy the spring and the sunshine. There had been times in the five years he'd been in the service of Wellington and later, Castlereagh, that Devon had wondered if it would ever be over.

He had spent so much time traveling between France and Prussia and so very little at his own home, that he'd worried about the neglect his estates were sure to have suffered. Not to mention the neglect his life had suffered. He had been much too much in the dark byways of Paris and London with less than savory characters. Sometimes he longed just to walk the fields at Stanton and watch the real processes of life unfold. His time in the government service assumed a nightmarish quality.

Not that France or Prussia were without their charms. But England was home. Nothing could change or disparage that. And he was ready, after leading what some had called a charmed existence, to spend some time with his own people. To try to find the threads of the life he'd left behind. To share a relationship with a woman for more than one night. He would be delighted if that woman was Louisa Drayton.

Devon Michael Christopher Hallot, Lord Stanton, Earl of Streiker, did not stop to question his intentions toward the lovely Duchess. She was an adult, of a good age, not some innocent miss, and a Peer of the Realm. In his experience, the combination of those circumstances and the right individuals could be extremely pleasant for both parties. In short, Devon could see the lovely Louisa in a small house he already owned in Kensington. The Season was almost upon them. With Louisa waiting upon his assignations, it promised to be exciting and unique.

That she was titled and rich meant little to him beyond that she was his peer and familiar with the ways of their counterparts. That she would have to be convinced to see him as something more than her horses. Ah! Now *that* would prove to be interesting!

The object of Devon's speculation finally reached the city after a long, hard journey. Louisa was careful to arrive in London at night, taking up residence at Roth Place near the park while most of London was about at some recreation. She wanted no fanfare for her arrival. Not yet at least.

It had been a long day and a half, traveling from Osbourne to London. The roads were crowded, dry, and dusty. The inn they'd spent the night at was full of ill-bred sportsmen and the food was bad. One of the horses had gone lame while they were on the road, making them wait while another was found and the horse replaced.

Beth was cheerful throughout and their companion, Jane Winslow, slept. The staff Louisa had brought from Osbourne grumbled. It was quite easily the worst excursion the Duchess had ever attempted. Still, she had the feeling it would be the best part of going to London.

Louisa looked out at the quiet English countryside sprouting green and awakening from its long winter slumber and wished a miracle would happen to save her from this fate. She wasn't a woman to hope for divine intervention but it seemed to be the only possible answer to the dread in her heart.

Even though they arrived in London late, her aunt's man of business was there to greet them. He introduced Louisa to the staff, as Mrs. Winslow and Beth were taken to their rooms. Louisa and Mr. Reresby sat in the library where a warm fire was lit. The night was cool, even though it was late in the year to be so. They exchanged pleasantries about her journey and the weather while Fleet, her aunt's butler, served them sherry. Mr. Reresby thanked him and the bland-faced butler left them alone.

Mr. Reresby had been the Dowager Duchess of Roth's advisor and confidant for close to twenty years. While in the service of that grand Madame, he thought that he had seen and heard nearly every strange and unusual idea. Yet the woman before him was now detailing the most outrageous plan he'd heard in twenty years.

The Duchess of Osbourne was the Dowager's favorite niece as well as her only goddaughter. He had already heard from Her Grace, the dowager, telling him that everything she had was to be at Louisa's disposal.

If it seemed a little strange, well, that was the aristocracy for you. It wasn't the first plot he'd helped to put in motion in that house! He could easily understand what drew the two women together. They were very much alike, both in face and personality.

"I suppose it seems a trifle odd." Louisa dared a look at the man from under her lashes.

Mr. Reresby shrugged. "Your aunt has never been a conventional sort, Your Grace."

"She never struck me as being odd," Louisa recalled. "Although I do recall Mama saying she hoped I wouldn't turn out to be like her since we were given the same name."

"The Dowager is an original," her faithful steward responded. "I believe I understand your predicament, Your Grace. What is it you require of me?"

"The most obvious parts, I suppose. Letting everyone know that we are in town for the Season, arranging my 'aunt's' itinerary. Everything you would normally do if Aunt Louisa were in town for the Season."

Mr. Reresby didn't mention that Her Grace, the Dowager Duchess, hadn't benefited Polite Society with her presence for nearly ten years. He assumed that, like her aunt, the Duchess of Osbourne would want results, not explanations. "Immediately. I shall do what is necessary, Your Grace. You may depend on me."

Louisa stood slowly, weariness etched into the delicate planes of her face. "Thank you, Mr. Reresby. I know I shall not fail so long as I have your help."

"Thank you for your trust, Your Grace." He stood and accepted her hand.

He was touched by her immediate faith in him. She had a great deal of dignity, like her aunt as well. He watched her slowly ascend the stairs with the housekeeper at her side. She was obviously exhausted but still doing what was expected of her. He sighed, knowing he could do no less to serve both ladies. The night was still long before him.

Beth sat wide-eyed on her bed, not believing that she was to have a Season! The pale pink room with its dainty tea rose effects and intricately carved four-poster bed assumed a fairy tale beauty. Just a fortnight earlier, she had been in the throes of despair. She blessed her father's memory that she had been given her Aunt Louisa. The lady in question joined her in her chamber after everything was in place for their introduction to society on the next day.

"You look happy," Louisa remarked, seeing her niece's radiant face.

"Happy? Oh yes, I am indeed. But I am also well aware that there is a job to do here, Aunt. I won't fail you."

"Fail me?" Louisa smiled and sat down beside her on the rose-embroidered comforter. "What do you mean?"

"I mean that I know I have only a short time to find a husband that meets with Mama's expectations. You were generous enough to give me a chance to find someone not so odious as the Viscount. I appreciate your help and I will do everything I can to find someone as quickly as possible. Betty has told me more than once how you loathe London."

Louisa laughed at the militaristic bent of her niece's thoughts, then kissed her forehead and touched the guinea-gold curls. "Good night, Beth. Sleep well. We have the beginning of an exhausting Season coming up on us tomorrow. Try to have a little fun, hmm? I did not bring you here just to marshal your campaign for the right husband. I want you to enjoy yourself. I don't loathe London nearly as much as I love you."

"Thank you, Aunt Louisa. Isn't it odd that the Dowager Duchess' name is Louisa as well?"

"Not really," she replied. "I was named for her. It is a common family name on our maternal side. I am the fifteenth Louisa in our family. Go to sleep now."

Louisa left her with a smile but her eyes welled with tears she'd promised herself she wouldn't shed when she thought of her brother, Michael. Beth's animated face was so like his. Her eyes were the same color as his.

She was glad the war was over, thankful that they had won. But there had been so much loss. Andrew's father was dead. Michael was missing. So many others. She was tired, she told herself, and dusty. She would wash and seek her own bed. Tomorrow was an important day for her as well.

It had been four years since she'd been in London. She'd had no intention of ever returning and truly only the most dire circumstances could have induced her to do so. That was why she'd given the townhouse to Andrew with an easy heart.

She hated London, the parties and the gossip. All she wanted to do was go back home. But there was Beth to consider and so she forced herself to remain. It would do her no good to relive old memories. Her father had taught her that. She missed his easy companionship. It seemed that she had been alone forever.

When her maid, Marie, had finally finished putting everything in order and the lamp was turned down in her gold and blue room, Louisa was left to her thoughts. Most were not what she wanted them to be. Some, like the handsome face of Lord Stanton, kept her company into the night. She went to sleep listening to the almost forgotten sounds of town, the call of the Watch, and the sound of laughter in the street.

Miles Cuthbert, Lord Haverly, sat uncomfortably in a stiff-backed chair watching his nephew finish his toilette. His gouty leg hurt abysmally but he had insisted on being moved to Devon's bedroom. "So the Duchess is as capable as the Duke always said she was! Andrew's mother was always a featherhead. Harry was no better! How could we expect more from the lad?" He waved away the offer of a pillow for his leg. His man, Farsley, sighed and stood back.

When Devon had returned from Osbourne and related his experience to his uncle, Lord Haverly had really had his own beliefs confirmed. He had met Louisa only once but he had been astounded by her very rare combination of intelligence and beauty. "One can only wonder how she has kept Bertie and Reggie there all these years without going mad," he remarked caustically. "I am glad to hear she has them under control. I should hate for that pair to try to find refuge here with me."

"I should have liked to have wrung all their necks, including Andrew's," Devon told him sincerely. He finished tying his cravat. His valet, on loan from Lord Haverly, since his own man had not had time to reach London before him, helped him into his exquisitely cut coat.

He had planned on going immediately to Stanton but that had changed when he had met Louisa. Since that happy occurrence, Devon found he could not find it in himself to think of anything but returning to that Lady's side. Those deep blue eyes promised so much. He wanted to talk with her, touch her again . . . under other circumstances.

He had dispatched a servant with flowers to her residence in town immediately upon his arrival. A hot bath had perked him up after the exhausting ride. From that time on, he had been restless to see her.

"So you mean to court the Duchess yourself, eh?" Lord Haverly chuckled. "I have heard, from Bertie, of course, that she cares more for that big horse of hers than any man."

Devon smiled as he placed his hat rakishly upon his head. "Being a tolerable judge of fine horseflesh," he drawled, "I can well understand her feelings. It is a magnificent beast."

"But that won't stop you trying, will it? She'll lead you on a merry chase, Devon."

The hazel eyes smiled with his mouth. "I have always been very good at hunting, uncle."

Miles laughed again. "You have always been very good at getting what you want."

Devon agreed silently with an acquiescing nod of his head. He took his leave of his uncle and hailed his driver and coach. The night was still young. He intended to spend the best part of it with Louisa.

It was only slightly after midnight when Lord Stanton finally admitted defeat. No one had seen hide-nor-hair of the lovely Duchess or her young niece. He'd had his man present his compliments with flowers to the butler at the Osbourne townhouse. The butler had squinted out at him with a jaundiced eye and told Devon's representative that there was no Duchess occupying the townhouse at that time.

Devon had given the returned flowers to a little girl in the street then they'd set off to find the Duchess.

He ended up at White's with a good glass of French brandy in his hand. Where could she be? Staying with friends rather than at her townhouse? It seemed unlikely she would not take advantage of her own residence! Yet he couldn't doubt the look of disgust on the butler's face. *Where was she?*

It was possible that she'd been delayed on the road. She was traveling with a large entourage. Delays occurred. She could even have been in an accident of some kind. He considered riding out towards Osbourne. If Louisa had been injured or simply been waylaid by a broken wheel or a lame horse, she might be glad of his company. No matter, he would not be seeing her that night.

Devon looked up from his doldrums when he heard loud voices enter the club. A group of young bucks, so drunk they were scarcely able to stand, stumbled into the room. One of them was Andrew. Devon swallowed his brandy and went to speak with him. If anyone knew where the Duchess was, it would be that young pup.

"Good evening, yer lordship," Andrew said with a drunken lisp.

"Good morning might be more like it," Devon told him.

Andrew glanced at the clock on the wall. "I wouldn't know. Can't see the clock, you know!"

His friends laughed with him at his fine joke. Devon sat them all down in chairs and ordered drinks for them.

"Decent of you," Andrew told him. "I thought you didn't like me."

"I don't like you," Devon replied honestly. "But I need some information from you."

Andrew leered at him. "You want to know the way to Louisa's heart?"

"I want to know where she's staying in town."

"Staying?" Andrew glanced around the room. "I hadn't thought of it! You don't suppose she's staying with me, do you?"

Devon thought the boy was having fun with him until he saw the look in his eyes. "Where else would she stay but at the townhouse?"

"My lord, I swear to you, if she is there, she did not say anything of it to me."

"So you don't expect her?"

"No! I should hope not! Imagine the crimp she'd put in my life? Perhaps I should go home in case she's already there! The harridan! I can't risk her cutting me off entirely until my birthday!"

"Easy." Devon put his hand on the boy's shoulder. "I just came from there. She's not there."

"But where else could she mean to stay if not with me?" Andrew wondered plaintively.

"She must have a friend in town," Devon speculated.

"Cousin Louisa? She gave me the townhouse because she would never use it. She doesn't know a soul."

"She doesn't mean to let a house, Andrew," Devon interposed. "Think, man!"

Andrew wrinkled his forehead but there was obviously too much alcohol in his brain to think of anything useful. "I can't, my lord."

His other friends were all but passed out around him. Devon took out a card and put it into Andrew's coat pocket. "If you hear from her, let me know."

Andrew grinned. "You are right after her, ain't you?"

"Be a good boy now, Andrew. I'll hail your carriage for you."

"No carriage," Andrew told him. "Just call a hackney."

Devon shook his head and left White's, instructing the doorman to hail a hackney for Louisa's cousin. He took a deep breath of the night air then rapped on the top of his own carriage to wake his driver.

"Let's go home," he said to the sleepy-eyed tiger. "We're wasting our time out here tonight."

Devon looked out of the window as they drove back to his home. The stars looked down at him through a murky haze. He asked of them the question that was foremost in his mind: *Where was Louisa?*

The watery sunshine peeked into Louisa's room, glittering on the gold threads in the dark blue draperies and making shadows on the walls. She looked around herself slowly and realized that she was sleeping in her aunt's bedroom. She had been allowed there only a few rare times as a child, but she recalled thinking that the drapes matched her aunt's eyes.

She realized that it was true.

With a sense of curiosity she wanted to dampen but found she could not, she donned her robe and went to the window. The scene below was full of life and color. Red and black curricles vied in the street with shiny black coaches. The finest horses in the world pranced and snorted, drawing their masters along through the rush and rabble. Merchants hawked their wares and liveried servants were on their way to do their errands. Dogs yapped at their heels and were quickly kicked away.

A few ladies with their many shaded parasols, their skirts flirting with the breeze, walked along the street. Gentlemen tipped their hats and smiled, flirting with their eyes and their words. Across from the house, she could see the beginning green of Hyde Park. The newly sprouted flowers waved their delicate heads. It wasn't a scene she wanted to find attractive, certainly not *exciting*, but there was a flutter in her stomach.

"She will be ready soon enough, Miss." Betty, Louisa's maid, pushed her way into the room with Beth at her side.

"That's all right, Betty," Louisa said, stepping away from the window. "Good morning, Beth."

"Aunt, you have been sleeping forever!" Beth spoke quickly, coming to perch on the arm of a chair. The sunlight picked out the tracing of pink flowers in her day dress and made her hair a golden halo around her excited face.

"I tried to tell her you'd be wanting your chocolate," Betty grumbled, putting the silver tray on the table near Louisa.

"This is fine, Betty." Louisa smiled, feeling her own spirits lift with her niece's enthusiasm. "Feeling eager?"

"Is it not glorious, Aunt Louisa?" Beth asked. "We are in London!"

"Yes, my dearest," Louisa agreed, sipping her chocolate. "But in London, no one fashionable rises before ten. And one does not go out on the street until two or three."

"Must we wait?" Beth pouted.

"As a matter of fact, we shall not wait. As the dowager, I shall be going forth somewhat earlier. I shall have to be made up from now on, however. The masquerade must be complete."

"So you mean to go through with this craziness?" Betty demanded in the tones of a long trusted servant.

"Oh, Aunt, must you?" Beth wondered, her blue eyes huge. "There would be ever so much more for you to do at your own age."

"And ever so many more problems, Beth. I do not want to appear vain, my love, but I also know the appeal of a large fortune. I am not interested in being chained to any man. I am happy with things as they stand."

"You sound ancient, Aunt!" Beth smiled. "But if you are so determined—"

"It's foolishness." Betty shook her head. "I may help you but I will not condone it. What if you are found out, Your Grace? Think of the ridicule!"

"We had best not be found out then, Betty," Louisa replied rationally. "With everyone doing their part, there is no reason to fear, I think. Are we set?"

Betty grimaced. "We have one of the... dresses... ready for you. And the face paint."

"Then let us create the role I must play." Louisa nodded cheerfully, though she was not certain her heart was totally in it.

She did want to be young, but she also wanted to be free. Not that she was so much worried about her own determination to be so. There was not a man who could entice her away from all that she possessed. She didn't want a crowd of gentlemen hovering around her as they did at Osbourne. The plan had come to her when a young gentleman, staying at her home for a weekend, continued to pay court to her. She had suggested that he look at Beth who was much his own age but he only shook his head and tried to kiss her.

At twenty-two, she was not so old that her face was unpleasant to look at and her fortune was well known. This way was for the best. This way Beth would have her Season and find her husband, she reminded herself as she sat and watched her face disappear while the dowager took her place. It was a transformation aided by stage makeup Betty had obtained from a traveling troupe of actors. Her own fine skin was made to appear wrinkled and fragile, thin lines drawn from her eyes and corners of her mouth.

"We want you to appear older," Betty said, using a light touch, "but we want you to be aging nicely."

"Like ivory and lace," Beth added, intrigued by the process.

Louisa's own pale hair was easily disguised since it was almost a natural color for her newly advanced age. Betty powdered it just slightly to give more the appearance of having been dressed for that purpose. "There is nothing we can do for your eyes." Betty sighed, stepping back. "You'll just have to look down a bit. They're a dead give-away."

"I don't know," Beth disagreed, critically analyzing her aunt's face. "Your eyes are stunning but they are so near Great-Aunt Louisa's that it may not matter."

Betty did not correct her notion by explaining that twenty years changed more than just the color of a woman's eye.

With her pale gray walking dress, slightly out of fashion yet very elegant, pulled over her own lithe form, Louisa surveyed herself carefully. She looked older, yet not ancient, aging nicely, as Betty had remarked. They had planned for her to be constantly gloved and veiled in the sunshine so as to aid the ruse.

"Well." She sighed. "We shall see if we can convince everyone else that the dowager is here to present Miss Montgomery to society."

By the time Louisa and Beth had walked slowly down the long staircase, Mr. Reresby had already spread the word that the dowager was in town and would be presenting her great niece to society. He had also sent word back to Osbourne that Louisa had decided to leave her niece to her aunt's ministrations and had gone on to France. It was a popular thing to do with the war over. Everyone at Osbourne knew how the Duchess felt about town.

Jane Winslow was slowly going over the invitations when they reached her at the desk near the breakfast room. She shook her graying brown head and smiled, then closed her eyes in shock at Louisa's appearance. "Oh dear!" She took a good look at the Duchess. "You *have* gone through with it!"

"There is no other alternative," Louisa reminded the older woman.

Jane was a cousin of Louisa's father, whose husband had died a few years before. She was eminently discreet and trustworthy. Her husband had been in the military, an attaché who carried secret documents. Louisa often wondered if Jane had learned discretion and decorum at his feet.

All of Louisa's staff had lived with gentlemen hiding in the Duchess' bedroom and lounging around the estate, hoping to impress her. One young man had gone so far as to leap out of a tree onto her horse as she rode past. Nostradamus had made short work of him! She knew they would understand her ruse but she didn't want to put them in the position that they would have to lie for her.

"The question is, how do I look?" Louisa turned slowly for the older woman.

"Like your aunt, Louisa. But surely—"

"Come, Jane," Louisa encouraged brightly. "There is no other way. We both know it. Let us see, instead, if we can convince Beth to eat something before we show her to the world."

Chapter Four

Mrs. Winslow felt the tug of her conscience but bit her lip and followed the other two into the breakfast room. She knew Louisa well enough to know that she had made up her mind. Her cousin was stubborn to a fault but they had been close friends for many years. Louisa had taken her in when she had noplace else to turn. Jane felt she owed Louisa much more than loyalty.

Several more invitations had arrived and visitor's cards were being presented before they finished breakfast. All were told that the ladies would not be at home to visitors until the following day.

Louisa talked her niece into eating a sliver of toast and drinking a small cup of tea. She found her own excitement prevented her really doing justice to the magnificent breakfast the cook had prepared. Jane ate enough to make up for the two other ladies, not so careful of her own increasing girth now that food seemed to be the only enjoyment left to her. Besides, she was well past the excitement London represented and she wasn't the one dressed as a dowager aunt.

Beth had been at the window watching the traffic and remarking on the number of people about for long minutes while Louisa finished her tea and Mrs. Winslow did her best to finish her breakfast. The horses and shiny black carriage, complete with Ducal crest, were brought round to the front steps.

"Are we nearly ready, Aunt?"

"We are nearly ready, dear," Louisa assured her.

"I feel near swooning with anticipation," Beth declared, her eyes bright, feet nearly dancing to the door.

Louisa found she agreed, despite herself. She glanced into the huge ornate mirror near the stairs. It would be a major humiliation to be found out. Yet how could her plan fail? Who would dare to question that she was who she said she was? She had the name and the *accoutrement*. Even if they considered that she looked a trifle too young, well then dear Aunt Louisa was simply aging well. If she didn't recall every face that claimed to know her, she was a trifle forgetful. The plan was perfect!

She took a deep breath and forced herself to walk out of the heavy wood door that led to the street. Without looking to either side, she went slowly to the carriage, mindful of her age, using her ornate walking stick. The groom handed her inside the carriage and she sat back against the comfortable squabs. So far, so good!

Most of the fashionable people in the city were barely greeting the day when the dowager and her party swept into the establishment of Madame Duvall on Bond Street. They had already dropped Mrs. Winslow off at the circulating library to indulge her passion for adventure novels.

The Dowager Duchess 57

Louisa refused to consider that her companion might be afraid to be present for her first outing. They would not fail!

There were a few other customers in the elegant little shop but Madame left them at once when she spied the Duchess' arrival in her splendid coach. Her small black eyes recognized quality in the expensive clothes on the Duchess and her protégée. She hadn't missed the Ducal crest.

"Your Grace." She swept the Duchess a deep curtsy. "How may we serve you?"

"My niece will require several garments for both day and night, Madame," Louisa told the obsequious woman sternly. "We would like a few day dresses to take with us now and the rest delivered later."

"Of course, Madame." The dressmaker smiled and bowed, signaling one of her assistants as she did. "This is my first assistant, Angelique. She is gifted with her hands. She will take your beautiful niece to be measured and perhaps find a gown or two for your approval?"

"That is fine." Louisa signaled her footman who found her a slightly shabby chair to sit upon. "I shall wish to review everything."

"Of course! I shall give Mademoiselle my private attention."

Louisa simply inclined her head and sat, stiff backed on the edge of the chair. She was glad for her cane to hold in her gloved hands to disguise her shaking. Sitting with her hands in her lap did not seem to answer the problem.

"Try to stay awake, Aunt Louisa." Beth gave her aunt a quick kiss, careful not to muss the makeup, then skipped off behind the curtains.

Louisa did not turn her head but allowed her eyes the

freedom to roam that portion of the shop that she could see. The flowered draperies were faded but had new velvet tassels sewed onto them. The carpet beneath her feet had once had a pastoral scene that was now worn nearly away. In all, there was a genteel shabbiness about the place.

Madame had been highly recommended to Louisa by Andrew's mother. That woman was nothing, if not fashionable! Louisa would not have taken her advice on any other subject, but the woman would know where to shop. Especially when there was coin to spend!

Two gentlemen were seated in a far alcove. As she watched, a young woman with shining black hair ran from behind the curtains and approached them. She twirled for their inspection of a daring red gown that revealed more than it concealed, then reached across to kiss one of them. *Very* thoroughly.

Louisa started to look away, feeling very *de trop*, not certain if the young woman would care, but embarrassed nonetheless. Then she noticed the gentleman who wasn't being kissed. He was very good-looking, and very familiar as well. He had broad shoulders, a narrow waist, and an intelligent turn of his head. *Lord Stanton*. He looked very handsome in his dark blue coat. She felt she would know him despite the darkness in the area of the shop where he was seated.

He looked away from the heavy embrace as well. His face mirrored amusement as their glances collided. At once, he seemed to come to attention. She could see the lazy ambience leave him. His eyes searched hers then went quickly to follow the line of her dress. He took in all of her with a single look.

But what a look! She wished that she had a fan to cool her hot face while she urged her heart to resume its beating in her breast. She wished she'd worn her heavy veil but it hadn't seemed necessary in the modiste's shop. Panic seized her and almost caused her to run out of the establishment.

Slowly, she counseled herself. It was only her fear of recognition. He could not know her from just a glance. He had known her as a child but had only seen her once as an adult. She was not herself but her aunt. She moved her gaze along the room without acknowledging him.

That did not stop him. With a movement she felt rather than saw, he came to his feet and sauntered her way. Just as Beth burst from the dressing room wearing a pale blue muslin that set off the blue of her eyes.

"Well, what do you think? I think . . . well! Hallo!"

Louisa felt her heart drop. It would have been better for Beth to ignore the gentleman but she was already advancing towards him with a broad smile on her pretty face.

"Miss Montgomery." He bowed to her elegantly. "You are correct. The dress becomes you."

Beth blushed furiously. "I thank you, Lord Stanton. And I appreciate your opinion. Might I present my Great-Aunt, the Dowager Duchess of Roth?"

She moved gracefully towards the dowager's chair. "Aunt Louisa, this is Lord Stanton. We met at Osbourne before Aunt Louisa and I left for town. He is a friend of the late Duke, I believe."

Louisa inclined her head, trying to recall her role. Beth seemed born to it. She held out her hand to the gentleman who took her gloved fingers in his own much warmer, ungloved hand.

"Lord Stanton," she acknowledged his presence, keeping her voice a touch deep and throaty. Her hand grew warm where he touched it, her face even warmer.

"Your Grace." He bowed briefly over her hand. "I am in total humiliation before you. There was a trick of the light, I think. For one brief moment, I thought you *were* your niece, Louisa Drayton. You are very similar. Especially your eyes."

He didn't release her hand, which was not acceptable. He seemed to forget himself with her. She felt tiny beads of perspiration start on her forehead. "I appreciate your candor, Lord Stanton." Louisa slightly muffled her speech, wishing he would go away. "You are known to my niece, Louisa?"

"Ah, yes, briefly, though we knew one another as young children." He glanced at Beth. "I was introduced to this young lady by her eloquent beast. I was recently at Osbourne Park and made their acquaintance."

"How interesting." Louisa veiled her eyes with her lashes, barely glancing at him. She recalled Betty's words. He was distinctly staring at her, as though he could see through her disguise. And he had not released her hand.

"I think you may be acquainted with my uncle, Lord Haverly. I believe I have heard him mention your name."

"Perhaps," she agreed carefully.

Madame joined them momentarily to rave about Beth's dress. Her wiry frame moved between the gentleman and the Duchess. Her strangely shaded red hair bobbed up and down on her head as she talked.

"What must I do for an introduction, Devon?" The other gentleman approached, smiling at Miss Montgomery. He was not as tall as Lord Stanton and he was a great deal thinner but his eyes were very blue and his smile was kind.

Lord Stanton came back to himself and released the dowager's hand. "Excuse me, Chatty, this is Miss Montgomery and her Great-Aunt, the Dowager Duchess of Roth. Ladies, Sir Lawrence Chatham."

"Pleased to make your acquaintance." He nodded, taking the dowager's hand but looking at Beth's gold and pink beauty. "Miss Montgomery, I hope we shall meet at Countess Markland's rout tonight?"

Beth looked hopefully at Louisa, who lifted her chin a little higher. "We shall see, child. Now run along and finish your fitting. I am certain these gentlemen will excuse you."

"Not that any garment could make you more lovely," Lawrence added with a wistful sigh.

"Now then!" Madame called to them. "A woman's garment is *very* important. She is who she wants you to see."

Louisa was disconcerted to find Lord Stanton's eyes fastened on her face as Madame pronounced her fateful words. She looked at him askance and he smiled brilliantly, setting a flutter within her.

"Your pardon, Your Grace, but your resemblance to your niece is quite amazing."

"Beth?" She hoped to disconcert *him*, her heart pounding.

"No, ma'am. The Duchess of Osbourne. Surely someone must have remarked on it? It is most uncanny. Your eyes. The curve of your cheek. Your smile."

"Yes, quite." She sighed as though bored with the comparison. "Many have told me so, Lord Stanton. That is why she was named for me."

Devon inclined his head quickly. "Forgive me being so monotonous, Your Grace. I shall endeavor to be more entertaining the next time we meet."

With that he bowed slightly and took his leave. Sir Lawrence fumbled his goodbyes and returned to his paramour at the other end of the shop. Madame followed quickly as she wrangled with the pair for even a farthing that Sir Lawrence owed on his dressmaker's bill.

Beth's eyes were dancing with mischief when she emerged wearing a golden-yellow walking dress. "Have they gone, Aunt?"

"Yes, thank goodness! I was totally put out of countenance meeting him here! Imagine! He would be here the very first day. It was as though he *knew*."

"I am sure he did not," Beth whispered. "He simply wanted to meet you."

Louisa shook her head and rapped her cane on the floor as Uncle Bertie did. "Go on, child. Finish quickly, if you please. I find myself growing fatigued."

"Your great age, no doubt," the girl replied cheekily before she danced off into the next room.

Louisa rejected the golden-yellow dress, too bright, but chose four others, including a turquoise gown that had been made for another. Madame assured them the lady would not be able to wear it because of a great tragedy in her family. Madame did not say that the tragedy was that her client could not pay her bill.

Beth fell in love with a simple white, almost gossamer creation that floated on her as she walked.

"Yes, we shall take that one as well. When will the others be ready, Madame?"

"I shall send on the *accoutrement* later today, the rest by the end of the week."

Louisa nodded. "That will do nicely."

"Does that mean," Beth queried, "that we shall not be able to go out again after tonight, for the remainder of the week?"

"If what I believe will happen tonight, happens, it will take that long for you to catch your breath."

Beth smiled. With a force of will she kept herself from jumping with anticipation into the coach beside her aunt. Everything was so splendid!

Louisa sat beside her niece, watching for Lord Stanton's form as they left the dressmaker's shop. She did not want to appear nervous but the man made her uneasy. It *was* as though he had seen through her charade. If they met again, she would have to be prepared.

But he was not waiting outside the shop. She chided herself for fretting unnecessarily. Everything would run smoothly. She *was* the Dowager Duchess!

Mr. Reresby had left word with Fleet that he wanted to speak with the Duchess alone when they returned. The butler gave them his message then bowed and left them.

Beth excused herself, and Louisa, despite her discomfort in her chosen costume, went to meet with him in the library. It was best to get accustomed to being the dowager anyway. No one needed to see Louisa Drayton staying at the townhouse when she was supposed to be in France.

"Do you think Mr. Reresby knows the truth, Louisa?" Mrs. Winslow wondered. Her face was almost comically exaggerated in fear.

"For a fact, Jane. I told him." Louisa nodded calmly. "It was necessary to obtain his help. I could not be the dowager without him."

Mrs. Winslow shook her head. "Whatever you think is best, dear." Then she retreated to her own room with her books and her chocolates.

Louisa sighed, watching Jane's stout form depart. It would do her no good to get cold feet now, she considered briefly. Besides, she was made of sterner stuff. Stanton might think the dowager's resemblance to her niece amazing but that was as far as he would get in unmasking her.

She took a deep breath then swept into the library. "Mr. Reresby," she greeted him as he stood to meet her.

"Your Grace." He stood, his mouth open, staring at her. "Excuse me, but you are so like your aunt—"

"So I have been apprised," she replied dryly. "My disguise is obviously a success."

She could not have said why this success perturbed her some little bit. It made no sense as she had planned it so carefully since she found that she must give Beth a Season in London. Had she expected to be found out? She found herself wondering crossly while she poured tea for herself and Mr. Reresby after the housekeeper had left them with the tray. Was it simply vanity that it had taken so little to make her look twenty years older than herself? She had never thought of herself as being a vain woman.

It was to be blamed squarely on Lord Stanton's broad shoulders, she decided finally. He had simply discomfited her with his ill-bred staring and holding her hand too long. It was nothing else.

"I should say so, Your Grace. Everything is in place, as you requested. Your friends, *ahem*, your *aunt's* friends, were pleased and excited to hear that you were in London. That is—"

"That is all right, Mr. Reresby." Louisa smiled, careful to move her mouth slowly as not to upset her face paint. It felt as though it were drying and cracking. "If you are confused, and *you* know the truth, Society will certainly accept me."

"Do you know how long you mean to remain in town, Your Grace?" He took his tea from her, trying not to stare at her face. He wanted to congratulate her again on the remarkable image she had created but refrained, as she seemed to be withdrawn. But it was truly astounding!

"Until we find Miss Montgomery a husband, Mr. Reresby. Not a moment longer."

"Very good, Your Grace." He inclined his head. "Please inform me if there is anything further I can do for you or your niece."

"We appreciate your efforts, Mr. Reresby. I believe we shall attend the Countess Markland's rout tonight." Louisa made her decision. The sooner Beth was launched into society, the sooner she could begin to find the right gentleman. "We did receive an invitation?"

"The Countess is well known to your aunt, Your Grace." He approved the decision heartily. "Her invitation was the first to arrive. She will be eager to receive you. Her friendship with Princess de Lieven will ensure vouchers to Almack's for your niece. Shall I write your acceptance?"

"Oh yes, Almack's. I had nearly forgotten." Louisa sighed. "That is an important consideration. Thank you. And yes, you may write our acceptance."

"My pleasure, Your Grace." Mr. Reresby accepted her gratitude with flustered delight. "Are there any other invitations you wish to accept?"

Louisa stood and shook her head. "Let us make it over the first hurdle, Mr. Reresby. Then we shall decide."

He nodded. "Exactly, Your Grace."

She left him there, determined that she would take off the makeup and be herself for a short while anyway. Surely there could be no harm in that while she was in her own room?

A messenger was sent with Her Grace's acceptance for the evening's entertainment while Louisa removed her makeup and rested in her rooms. Beth was also admonished to rest but it seemed unlikely that she would be able to do so.

Louisa remembered her first and only rout, a sad crush with too many people and nothing to eat or drink. Several of the young ladies had fainted. A few had been sick. Many had left in disgrace, their white gowns ruined. Louisa had merely been frightened and alone. Gawky and unsure, she'd stood to one side with the other unfortunates who were socially acceptable but unable to make the transition from schoolroom to ballroom. She'd kept her eyes carefully trained on the floor.

The room had been abloom with color. The women had looked like beautiful flowers in their gowns while their jewels flashed in the light from the chandeliers. The men's faces had run together while she wondered who would offer for her.

A title wasn't important, her parents had told her. All that had mattered was finding the right husband for her. But Louisa was tall, taller than many of the gentlemen. And she had a tendency to dance across their feet. She spent most dances watching from the sidelines. When a gentleman did approach, she was nervous and stuttering in her speech. It didn't make for many proposals of marriage.

Louisa might have become more accustomed but her mother's light cough had become consumption after reaching London. They'd had to return to Osbourne after only a month. She'd died only a few weeks later. Her father, grief stricken at his wife's death, hadn't pressed Louisa to try again on the marriage mart. He'd been content to let her stay at home and look after him and the estate.

Her brother, Michael, had joined the military. He had married Alice and conceived Beth between campaigns. He'd never had any interest in the estate and said as much to Louisa and their father. Sadly, he hadn't had much interest in his only daughter either. Louisa was trying to make up as much for his lack of regard and affection as for Alice's greedy nature.

Betty came in with some light refreshment, informing her that Beth had been getting ready for an hour. "She'll be ready before you, that's for certain. Especially with all we're going to do to you."

"Stop muttering, Betty. We are going to see this through. It is for the best."

"Whatever you say, Your Grace," the maid replied huffily.

Louisa sighed and sat down in front of her mirror. She was sorry she had tried to sleep. She didn't feel rested. Recalling her mother's death and the pall it had cast on them all, reminded her of how truly terrible it had been to be in those close rooms with gentlemen who didn't find her attractive.

She shuddered again at the memory. Beth wouldn't have that problem, thank heaven! She was as graceful and personable as she was beautiful. No thanks to Alice or her brother, Beth would have no difficulty finding a gentleman to offer for her.

It was faster becoming the dowager the second time. She might even continue to wear the terrible face paint after she returned to Osbourne! It would keep all the gentlemen away. Her future would be secure in its solitude. She grimaced at herself and Betty sighed.

Without meaning to, she thought of Lord Stanton, wondering what there was about him that she found so attractive. For she did, despite the fact that she knew she should not. It endangered her deception and Beth's future.

Yet, he *was* attractive to her. Monstrously so. There was probably not a lady of the *ton* that did not wish to be with him. Those eyes, so quick and intelligent, so evilly framed by those thick, dark lashes. One could imagine how he looked asleep, his features softened, vulnerable. One could also imagine the hearts he had trod upon. There was no innocence in his beauty.

"There you are," Betty remarked. "Ruined, and I hope, happy with it."

"Thank you," Louisa replied calmly, putting those other wayward thoughts from her. "I believe I shall wear the gray satin tonight."

Betty helped her into the dress. The material was beautiful. It shimmered in the light. The style was from a generation before but it did nothing to detract from Louisa's slim waist and firm, athletic body. Betty kept her own council on *that*. If the Duchess knew, she'd certainly order padding as well. It was the outside of enough that she wore such a terror with a closet full of perfectly good gowns at Osbourne. And her beautiful skin and hair! It was enough to give the husky maid a heart palpitation!

Beth paced restlessly downstairs waiting for her aunt. Jane waited with her; reminding her young charge from time to time that patience was a virtue. When Beth finally saw her descend, she tended to agree with Betty's assessment of the gown but kept her thoughts to herself. What could it hurt for her aunt to be somewhat attractive?

"Do you plan to beat off any suitors you do not approve of?" Beth asked, seeing the elegant black cane again in Louisa's gloved hand.

"It is something to do with my hands," Louisa told her. "I find that I am in need of a diversion."

At once Beth was all concern. "Is it terrible, Aunt Louisa?"

"Not at all," Louisa replied with a smile at her lovely niece. "Shall we go?"

The Dowager Duchess 69

* * *

A few hundred of the Countess Markland's closest friends were pushed into a space meant only for a fraction of them. But they were too gay and eager for gossip to stay away.

London was in the beginning throes of a mad celebration that began when news of Napoleon's defeat had begun to trickle back to war-weary England.

To make matters worse, Prinny had come and gone only recently as they arrived and the windows were only then being opened. The rooms were still stuffy and close. Ladies breathed shallowly in their stays and gentlemen attempted to keep up their appearance of cool aloofness though many cravats had disastrously wilted.

As a first appearance into Society, it left much to be desired. It was difficult, in the crush, to tell one white-gowned Miss from another. Or for that matter, Louisa found quickly, one face from another. She and Beth stayed together but the line moving up the staircase seemed to have stopped, leaving them stranded in a crowd of gentlemen.

Louisa tapped her foot impatiently, worrying about her face paint melting down her neck in the heat. She looked for an opening to move further up the stairs and into a room. Preferably, she thought crossly, a room with an open window.

Beth on the other hand was enchanted by everything. Her eyes roamed over the *beau monde* as they spoke about the latest *ondit*. She looked down into the foyer at the lovely colored gowns as the ladies crowded together, waiting for the stairway to clear.

"Lord Stanton!" Louisa heard Beth exclaim but she could

not turn to see the man, since the crowd pushed her against the rail.

"Your Grace. Miss Montgomery. It is quite a crush tonight, is it not? If you will allow me to assist you, I believe I see a break in the throng."

Stanton had reached a level with them. He smiled into Louisa's face. The smile stirred her and made her angry. She did not want to feel that catch in her throat at his nearness. Nor did she want to notice that the emerald stickpin in his cravat was no greener than his eyes. He was garbed very plainly contrasted to most of the crowd. But his shoulders were very broad beneath the black evening jacket. She knew they owed nothing to padding. The man was solid and muscular. The dazzling white of his shirtfront appeared inescapable before her startled eyes.

"Oh, we shall be delighted—er—shall we not, Aunt Louisa?" Beth caught her impulsive speech. Her blue eyes danced in the candlelight.

"Of course," Louisa agreed, despite her worries about the gentleman. Anything not to continue to stand in that mass!

With Lord Stanton in the lead, the crowd parted for them to climb slowly up the stairway. Louisa found herself close behind him, not wanting to be lost in that humanity but careful not to touch him. She held tightly to Beth's hand just behind her. She did not notice when the group in front of Lord Stanton stopped abruptly. She would have walked directly into him but he half turned, quickly putting out his hands to steady her.

Louisa was glad of the face paint to disguise the red she knew would be there. What was there about the man that made her fall into him at every turn? It was infuriating. It was exasperating. And touching him brought back those feelings that she had experienced at Osbourne.

He looked at her carefully, moving his hands away from her waist almost as swiftly as he'd put them on her. Louisa did not look up at him to see the puzzled frown on his handsome face.

When they reached the top, the rooms opened before them. Beth thrilled at the sight of more gentlemen and their ladies. The sparkling light of the chandeliers danced on the ceiling. Gowns of satin and silk in rainbow colors mixed with correct black coats and starched white collars crowding the floor. There was not a sign of empty space.

The strong perfume of unseen flowers filled the air along with the varied scents of sandalwood and jasmine. And a few smells that Louisa considered would have been better for a bath.

"Louisa!" A female voice called out, slightly husky in timbre and rich with allure.

Louisa turned to see an older lady bearing down on them through the crowd, the wave of gentlemen and ladies parting like the Red Sea before her Moses figure. Startled, she glanced up to find Lord Stanton's eyes quite thoroughly assessing her face. For a long moment, she stared back at him, only looking away when her friend reached her side. *What did he see?*

"Louisa! It is so good to see you, dear! An age! When did you arrive back in town? Why did you not let me know you were coming?"

If he was feeling any suspicions about the dowager, this would put them to rest! Louisa felt a smug smile on her face, something she couldn't seem to prevent no matter how she tried. If Lord Stanton wished to see her discomfited by the lady's appearance, he would be sorely disappointed.

Chapter Five

Like an actress born to the role, Louisa smiled and greeted Countess Markland. "It was so sudden. There was no time to do anything more than fly back to help my great niece."

"Oh yes." The Countess smiled at the young girl. "You may, of course, expect vouchers for Almack's but only if you promise that we shall have a nice long coze before the Season is over!"

"Of course, and thank you. Beth is so looking forward to her coming out. And Almack's! What young girl doesn't dream of making her debut there?"

Countess Markland preened behind her gaily painted fan. The light caught on the diamonds in her hair and around her throat. Her eyes went to Louisa's companion. "Ah, Stanton! How good to see *you* as well. We have not had the pleasure in far too long."

"Countess." He bowed over her gloved hand. "You are looking as lovely as ever."

"Liar!" She smiled. "But you do it so well! Did you come with the Duchess?"

"No." He glanced towards Louisa. "We met on the stairs, which I am very much afraid, Countess, are in serious danger of collapsing at this point."

"It is a press, is it not?" she agreed. "But it is a good way to see everyone at once and Prinny does love to come and run."

"And what do you hear of the Czar's sister?" Devon wondered.

"The Princess is coming to stay. With her *entire* entourage! Can you imagine? Dorothea has arranged everything. I should have made a ruin of the whole thing!"

"The Prince must be transported," he predicted, knowing the two did not get on.

Emily, Countess Markland shrugged. "Indeed. I see the Earl is looking for me. Louisa, recall your promise to me. Stanton, we shall expect to see you more now the war is over." The Countess disappeared in the sea of faces and garments that covered the room.

Louisa found herself wishing that it was over as easily as that but she knew it was only the beginning. She had to congratulate herself, however. If the Countess had thought that she was Louisa, Dowager Duchess of Roth, there would be no others who could come closer.

The Duchess and the Countess had once been great friends. Louisa knew she would not be able to have that coze with the Countess without giving herself away. But she would manage to be indisposed or busy when it came up. It would doubtless only be a few weeks. She could easily keep up the subterfuge for that length of time, couldn't she?

"Stanton!" A man edged from behind a marble pillar that was draped with velvet. "I have been looking for you." It was Andrew. His eyes lit up when he saw Beth. "Miss Montgomery! It is delightful to see you again." Suddenly, his eyes lost their sparkle and he glanced uneasily around the floor. "Where is The Dragon?"

"I beg your pardon?" Beth countered, wishing she could do or say something to keep him from his next words. He could, of a certainty, ruin everything.

"Your Aunt Louisa. She would not have left you here on your own! She must be here somewhere, ready to revile me for my clothing expenditures."

Indeed, anyone could see why this would be likely. He was the epitome of fashion with his cravat so high he could scarce turn his head. His pale blue satin breeches were fitted to his lean form and his silk stockings were molded to muscular calves. The sapphire stickpin matched the sapphire ring on his left hand.

"Rest easy," Devon said slowly. "She does not appear to be here at the moment. But have you made the acquaintance of the Dowager Duchess of Roth? She is escorting Miss Montgomery this evening. Your Grace, Lord Drayton."

"Your Grace." Andrew bent over Louisa's hand. He looked into her eyes and his eyes widened in his handsome face. "I say, you look a great deal like—"

"She has heard that tale earlier," Devon stopped him quickly. "I promised not to bore Her Grace with it again and I suppose I should save her from you as well."

"My thanks, Lord Stanton," Louisa said slowly. "Lord

Drayton. You look a deal like your uncle. I hope you are not as intemperate?"

Andrew blushed slightly and dared a glance at Beth, who was carefully studying her gloved fingertips. "My apologies, Your Grace. It was not my intention to offend. I am well acquainted with your niece. She is my cousin, by marriage. We sometimes do not view things the same way but I respect her very much."

"So I gather." Louisa found she quite enjoyed the young man's discomfiture. "The Dragon, as I believe you referred to her, is not here at present."

"She is at home with a head cold," Beth supplied, eager to help.

Louisa's gaze flew to her niece's face. *What was she saying?* Louisa was supposed to be abroad in France!

"Oh, truly?" Andrew smiled sincerely. "I am sorry. Please express my, ah, regrets to her that I could not see her this evening."

Lord Stanton listened to the exchange while studying the dowager's face. It was absurd how the likeness had haunted him since they had met. It was rude but he could not help staring, watching those summer sky eyes. They were so alike. It was uncanny. Even to the perfume he recalled from that day in the library at Osbourne. He had come to London to find Louisa. Instead, had found an older likeness that taunted him.

"I am anxious to reacquaint myself with your niece," Devon said to the dowager, keeping his eyes carefully on her own.

"She will no doubt be on her feet shortly," Louisa replied. There was no help for it. She would have to support Beth's rashly spoken words. She would have to send Louisa back to France as soon as she was well.

Devon inclined his head, his green eyes moving slowly over every aspect of her face. "I shall certainly call on her."

Louisa felt her heart drop like a stone in her chest. *Call on her?* She could not allow him to call on her! She could already see the suspicion in his face. If she had to revert to her true identity, then back to the dowager, it might seal it for him. He could not call on her!

"She will be leaving at once for the Continent when she is well," Louisa told him gruffly. "She doesn't like town anymore than I."

"But perhaps she will receive me before she leaves?" Devon persisted. "We are, after all, old friends."

Louisa glanced at Beth but the younger woman was too caught up in the music and the fascination of the people around her to lend her any support. "I cannot speak for her, Lord Stanton. But I do know she is eager to leave London."

Devon nodded, not wanting to press the point any further since the Dowager sounded anxious. "Allow me to introduce your niece to some of the eager young gentlemen who are anxiously awaiting her attention."

"Thank you." Louisa nodded as a group of young people crowded in close to them.

It was going to be difficult, she realized. Even more so than she had first considered. She hadn't thought of Lord Stanton being in London. She hadn't planned on Beth telling him that she was home with a head cold. If she allowed him to call on her, word would get out. They would be deluged with suitors for *her* hand rather than Beth's.

From what she'd heard of Stanton, he was definitely not seeking a wife. He could have something much more vile in mind than marrying her for her fortune. Men did have other needs. It would be a novelty to be approached for something less than an honorable proposal of marriage and the need of her fortune, she considered silently as the music swirled around her. Not that she would ever conceive of doing such a thing! She turned her mind back to her niece, far from such wayward thoughts.

It was easily apparent to Louisa's concerned gaze that Beth was a success. Young people crowded around her for an introduction. Several young men asked for permission to take her driving on the following day. Though the crush increased, Beth made her mark.

Louisa was pleased to see Beth take it all in stride, speaking with them all equally. Especially Andrew. That young man seemed to become immediately enamored of her niece. Louisa was not comfortable with this idea, but could do nothing about it at the time. She had taken note of their attachment at Osbourne but felt certain it would wither in the light of Beth's Season. Beth was a levelheaded girl. She would make an appropriate choice.

Stanton, she noticed with a sigh of relief, disappeared into the crowd after the first few moments. Bored to tears, no doubt. Even at her best, she would not be considered scintillating. Not when he could be with some *Incomparable* or a *Diamond of the First Water*. It was as well for her, she decided after her first feeling of disappointment had passed.

Yes, he was tall, impossibly good looking, and she was certain he could charm the birds from trees. But she did not trust him. Nor did she care for the intent way he had of looking at her, as though he could see through and beyond her illusion. She was not looking for Stanton's attention. She did not want him to find her irresistibly fascinating. She repeated that phrase over to herself as she chatted with strangers who knew her aunt.

She was far more comfortable with any of Aunt Louisa's

old friends. Even Colonel Parker, who had been one of her aunt's suitors, had been easily drawn into the deception. The Colonel was attentive and a ready companion. His thick shock of white hair and fierce gray eyes matched his quick humor and razor-sharp observations.

His niece, Miss Annabelle Watson, who became instant friends with Beth, accompanied him. They were a perfect foil for one another. Beth with her golden hair and blue eyes and Miss Watson with her ink-black hair and green eyes. Louisa smiled to see them together in their white gowns. There was so much promise in their innocence and loveliness.

She was careful what she said to the Colonel in her guise as her aunt but she was not overly taxed by the effort. The Colonel and her aunt hadn't seen one another in some time and the man positively exuded conversation. When she didn't answer, he simply glossed over with his own memories of their times together. And every other time in history!

Unlike Stanton, who gave her the feeling that he was watching her, waiting for her to make a mistake, the Colonel was simple. Devon listened too carefully, stared too intently. It was ridiculous, of course. He did not know that she was anyone but her aunt, the dowager. Anything else was in her imagination.

Those green eyes were beautiful and veiled discreetly by his black lashes as they watched her. But he could not know the truth. He was just intrigued by the similarities between herself and her aunt. Nothing more, she reassured herself. She would have to be more confident. Her masquerade was a smashing success. Her aunt's contemporaries, most who hadn't seen her in ten or twelve years, had surrounded her. They had accepted her.

She knew enough about each one to keep up the charade. At least for a time. She and her aunt had corresponded regularly for years. Beth was so lovely and her personality as flawless as a summer sky. She would find the right gentleman long before they thought to question. And who, she asked herself, would ever dare to imagine that someone would impersonate the dowager?

Louisa yawned in the carriage as they made their way home through the dark streets of London.

"What a wonderful night!" Beth said for the hundredth time.

"Yes," Louisa agreed again, watching the streetlamps pass.

"All the gentlemen were so dashing, so handsome."

"Yes, dear." The sounds of the carriage and the horses resounded in the night.

"It will be difficult to choose, Aunt Louisa," Beth informed her quietly. "I had not realized how hard it would be."

"That is the idea," Louisa replied. "However, before you choose any of them, get to know them first. As with Andrew, all is not as it appears."

"You were flawless," Beth answered, changing the subject adroitly. She knew there was bad blood between her aunt and Andrew. Personally, she found him exciting and attractive. He just needed a firm hand.

"They did seem to believe I was Aunt Louisa."

"That is not surprising since you look so much like her. The painting in the study could be you," Beth informed her. "I am sorry about the slip, though, Aunt Louisa. Do you think Lord Stanton will call?"

"If he does, we shall deal with it then," Louisa told her firmly. "All that matters is that you have enough time, Beth.

Make the best choice you can. I believe we can fool everyone until then."

"I do not know how to thank you," Beth said slowly. She pushed the music and the feelings Andrew had stirred in her from her mind. "That you should go to so much bother—"

"It is nothing, really. If it was not for that Lord Stanton—"

"He is delightfully interesting, is he not?"

"No, he is not," Louisa answered flatly. "He is a nosy busybody. He makes me uncomfortable. I wish he would go back to France or wherever he came from."

"You are just angry that he tried to kiss you when he fell on the floor." Beth smiled. "I heard the maid talking about it at Osbourne."

"That was the outside of enough," she agreed. "And we should not be discussing it. But it is more than that. I think he is planning some way to expose me."

"Aunt Louisa!"

"It is true. I find his presence unnerving."

Beth considered that perhaps those feelings were exactly what her aunt needed in her life. Her Aunt Louisa's life was all too planned and exacting for her taste. Where was the adventure? Where was the excitement?

She refrained from remarking on it, going to her bed quickly when they returned to the townhouse. After all, Aunt Louisa had managed her life for many years *without* her help. And it seemed she might need some help with her own affairs.

Louisa had been certain that when her head hit the pillow she would be asleep until late the next day. However, she was awake and up with the gray morning, watching the street cleaners from her window, sighing over the children that ran ragged through the streets.

She looked at herself in the gilt-edged mirror. The paint was not yet applied and her hair was still down around her shoulders. Some of her early disappointment in her unconventional looks surfaced in her heart and she sighed. Her lips were too wide and her face not cherub-like at all. Instead, she was tall and angular. The Duke had called her 'handsome,' but she would have given much to be blessed with a round face and a petite form.

Louisa folded the faded pink robe she wore more closely about her. The morning was cool. Her robe had seen better days but it was serviceable, hugging her slender form like a gentle hand. What she wouldn't give to be at Osbourne Park, riding out on the fields in the mist with the sweet smells of morning! It was really the only place she could lose herself.

An idea, rather desperate and dangerous, formed in her mind. She tried to push it aside but the more she tried, the more it clung.

She could ride in the park. She would have to be careful and be out early before the fashionable crowd. No one of any consequence rode in the early morning. If she dressed in such a way as to not draw attention to herself, it began to appear possible. It seemed she had asked Fleet to have the young stable boy ready a mount before she had realized what she was doing.

What could it hurt? She questioned herself as she dressed without Betty's help. The maid would have fussed and grieved until Louisa would have given up on the idea. The morning beckoned and she was going out. It would not be a ride at home but it might be a way to keep her sanity until they could leave London. The wind would blow away some of the cobwebs that had begun to form in her brain.

The mare they brought round for her was fresh and ready for the exercise. She was not Nostradamus but she was excited and obviously glad to be out. Louisa spread her wine colored riding skirt around her. The mare would be far easier to control than the huge stallion. She nodded to the stable master as she took the reins in her hands and they were off.

She had a few afterthoughts about taking a groom with her on the ride but he would have complicated her already complex world. She just wanted a few moments of peace in the park with only her horse and the greenery for company. Time to think and to re-focus her attention on the task at hand.

The streets were devoid of any fashionable conveyance as she started on the trail past the beds of yellow daffodils and the damp shrubbery. Some street vendors hawked their wares but it was servants who answered. Their masters were still fast asleep for the most part. It would be hours before they thought of dressing and going out.

Louisa kept the mare to the paths, her pace sedate, her mind wandering with the clouds above the treetops and the birds fluttering in the bushes. The morning sunshine was warm and sweet and her fears seemed like nothing in the breeze.

She heard a horse galloping quickly along the path behind her and moved carefully to one side, not wanting to hinder the rider. The mare snorted a little nervously but stayed where Louisa guided her. To her surprise, the horse behind her began to slow. When she turned to look behind her, she groaned. Her stomach did a nervous flip.

It was *him*, of course.

The Dowager Duchess 83

"Good morning, Your Grace." Lord Stanton smiled his greeting.

His hair, so carelessly kissed with gold, was a trifle windblown, giving his face a devilish quality. His dark coat was carefully cut to allow for the width of his shoulders while his buckskin breeches were molded to his long legs. In short, his appearance was guaranteed to create a tumult in the female breast.

"Good morning, Lord Stanton." If there was a sigh of frustration in her voice, she could not help it. She felt haunted, hunted by him.

"I hope you are feeling more the thing today?"

"Yes, I am quite improved. Thank you for asking."

"I would be happy to accompany you," he volunteered.

"I would not want you to trouble yourself, my lord," she replied distantly, hoping he would simply leave her there. Perhaps if she were unforgivably rude, he would take the hint.

"No trouble at all, Your Grace. Indeed, I would feel remiss if I did not since you are unfamiliar with the city and have not been well."

"As I said," she repeated pointedly. "I am quite well now, Lord Stanton. And I did make my bow here. I am not unfamiliar with the city."

"Yet you have never visited since, Your Grace," he began, nudging his horse into a place beside her own on the path.

"There is no need to accompany me," she assured him.

Lord Stanton's green eyes narrowed on her face. "One would think that you were attempting to cut me, Your Grace."

Louisa shook her head. She didn't want to ride with him but she didn't want to give him any reason to be suspicious of her either. "I would be grateful for your company, my lord."

He laughed. "That might be doing it a bit brown, Your Grace. But I am enchanted by your company."

Louisa felt a sharp stab of pleasure at his words. She looked away at the shafts of sunlight through the trees that only minutes before had brought her such joy.

"I know you are angry," he continued as she moved her mare along. "I would be wiling to go to great lengths to gain your forgiveness."

"What is there to forgive?" she began, shaking her head. Her voice was husky. Too much like the dowager's. She cleared her throat.

"My neglect of you. I knew you were in town but did not call on you. I would very much like for us to become better acquainted." Though nothing could be further from the truth, he was loathe to admit that he wouldn't have been able to find her if he hadn't stumbled across the dowager and Miss Montgomery. When the younger woman had revealed that her aunt was still in London, he could tell it was unwitting. Was Louisa trying to avoid him?

"We have very little in common," she assured him, refusing to rise to the blatant invitation in his velvet voice.

"I believe that you may find we have much to discuss," he continued, nonplussed. "For example, I would like to inquire about the mishap with the ladder and the beast. You seem none the worse for the experience."

"I might say the same of you, my lord," she retorted, feeling his eyes roam the length of her and back with more attention than could have been warranted. She wondered what more she could say to make him understand that he was not wanted. The man was nothing if not persistent.

And she was nothing if not intrigued by what he saw in her.

"I could only wish that such were the case." He shook his head ruefully.

"You seem well now," she added quickly, her eyes scanning his lean, athletic form. "You should never have attempted to stand so soon after. Is it your back?"

"Alas, no," he answered with a heavy sigh. "My heart."

"Your—your," she stammered, uncertain, caught between humor and anxiety. "What a load of rubbish!"

She saw the evil twinkle in his eye as he laughed. "Not at all, Your Grace. When I rose from my deathbed to find you gone, I thought I should perish on the stairs."

Had he *really* come to seek her out? "I believe your heart would take much more abuse than that, my lord! It could be your ego that is paining you. Or perhaps your conscience?"

"Perhaps," he agreed, amiably. "But you allow too much for the armor that surrounds my heart, Your Grace. It is really quite fragile."

"No doubt," she scoffed, "because it has rarely been touched."

They moved far to one side to allow a trio of fast-moving horses to pass them. Louisa smirked. So much for her theory that no one rode in the early morning!

"You must accept that I am sincere in my apology, Your Grace," he said quietly when the riders had passed them. The trees above them moved with the breeze. His eyes were steady on hers. "I would like to know you better."

His high-booted leg brushed her own through her skirt as the horses moved apart. Louisa felt the pulse in her throat double. "There is not much to know," she countered, starting back down the path. "And doubtless what there is to know, you would find rather boring."

"My visit to Osbourne Park told me many things about your abilities to manage an estate," he admitted, staying resolutely beside her. "But there are those things that only you can share with me."

"Such as?" she inquired briskly, ready to repel his blatant advance.

"Why you mean to plant barley in your fields instead of wheat and where you acquired the ingenious idea for the drainage field near the south bend."

"What?" She stopped short and stared at him, totally disconcerted to have been ready for an impertinence only to be consulted for her knowledge of *farming*. She did not know if she were glad or disappointed.

He placed his gloved hand on her horse's neck, bringing them closer as the mare snorted and tried to shy away from his bigger gelding. "And other questions as well," he enjoined. "May I call you Louisa? Are your eyes as blue by candlelight? Will you dance the waltz with me?"

The mare snorted again and threw her head back. It broke the long moment that Louisa studied his face, feeling a faint color rise up in her own.

Devon smiled as she looked away, seeing the beginning awareness in her eyes, wishing that her awareness were as strong and deep as his own for her. He knew that patience would be called for. Courting her promised to be a painful experience.

"I must return." She hedged away, starting back down the path the way she had come.

"I would like very much to accompany you and your niece to the Stephensons' ball this evening. If you are planning on attending?"

"I am leaving for Osbourne this very afternoon," she replied in a panic, biting her tongue as the words slipped out of her mouth. She was *supposed* to be leaving for the Continent!

Oh, but this was *supposed* to be easy! Of course, she had never tried to keep up so much subterfuge for quite so long with quite so many people! she reminded herself bluntly. It was what came of telling lies, even for the most noble of causes. All of her senses were alive to him. His hand on her mare, the way his eyes moved over her face. The manner in which he spoke that invited closer confidences. Everything urged her to spend more time with him.

"So soon?" His eyes entreated and she found she could not look away.

His words tugged at something inside of her. She did not want to feel anything for this man, she reminded herself again. Yet, there she was, mesmerized, like the bird and the snake. "I have delivered my niece to my aunt for chaperonage. I do not wish to remain in London any longer. My estate—"

"—will surely run along beautifully with your dedicated steward, Your Grace. Stay—just a day or two. Allow me to show you something of London. I know you have not been in the city for many years."

Louisa's heartbeat doubled. She knew her cheeks were pink beneath her riding hat. At that moment, it would have been glorious to be young and carefree. It would have been wonderful to be able to stay and see the city with him. But duty called and fear had encircled her heart.

She held her mare in check and shook her head. "I'm afraid personal business calls me away, my lord. Perhaps another time." She smiled quickly then let her mount carry her out of the park. Surely no gentleman would pursue a lady after that set down! Lord Stanton would not be looking out for her again.

Devon watched her ride away, knowing better than to follow, wishing that he did not. Her stiff back beneath the burgundy jacket was straight as a lance and did not invite company. He patted his horse's neck distractedly. That last should have frozen a lesser man!

Had there been a trace of wistfulness in her beautiful eyes? For just a moment, did she wish to stay with him? Not that it mattered. He would give her a day or two to regain her footing at Osbourne Park then he would follow and meet with her there. She would learn that he did not give up so easily.

Louisa looked back only once as the path she followed narrowed and turned away from her antagonist's searching eyes. He was not following. Thank heaven! It was for the best, she reminded herself. Beth was the important one here. If she didn't find a husband, Louisa shuddered at what waited for her young charge.

After all, she reminded herself, she wasn't young and she wasn't carefree, despite her wishing. She was a Duchess, twenty-two years old, responsible for a great estate. That would have to be enough for her. That *was* enough for her! She'd had her turn at finding the right man.

It was as well that she had put an end to any idea that he had about her living in the townhouse with the dowager and Beth. Especially since the thought that she might never see him again had begun to be more disturbing than that he might find a way to see her.

Fleet met her at the door, as she would have entered. "Your Grace," he said looking less than his usual dapper self.

"What is it, Fleet?" she demanded.

"The maid found it this morning as she cleaned."

"Found what, Fleet?" Louisa wondered if the man were ever going to come to the point.

"Someone has broken into the house and ransacked the library!"

Chapter Six

Mr. Reresby stumbled from the library as she approached, wringing his hands. "Oh, Your Grace! I'm afraid I did something-er-less than thoughtful when we found the library laid out in this manner."

It was difficult for Louisa to imagine Mr. Reresby doing anything without giving it serious consideration. "What is it?"

"I have sent for the authorities, Your Grace. I was that upset at seeing the library and I—"

"That's quite all right, Mr. Reresby," she returned, making for the stairs quickly. She understood the implication. The authorities would have to find the Dowager Duchess there in her place. She must change at once!

She was still unsettled from her ride with Lord Stanton and had hoped for a bath after taking the mare back to the stables. Everything would have to wait, however, as she flew to her rooms, telling Beth to fetch Betty at once.

them. Louisa and Mr. Reresby drew a collective breath. Fleet rested momentarily against the door.

Beth laughed. "What a treat! It was like the Circus, wasn't it, Aunt Louisa? Imagine that? Great-Aunt Louisa has found a treasure. Do you think she is on her way back with it right now?"

Louisa looked at Mr. Reresby who mopped his forehead with his handkerchief. "I'll see what I can discover about this—er—surprise, Your Grace."

Louisa thought about little else as she accompanied Mrs. Winslow and Beth on a trip to the jewelers to have a clasp repaired on Beth's sapphire bracelet. Jane had to ask her the same question more than once as they ogled hideously expensive jeweled peacocks and finely wrought silver.

The two other women laughed aloud at a rakish older gentleman and his exquisitely dressed paramour choosing a rather ostentatious emerald ring. Louisa reminded them of where they were in her best dowager voice then insisted that they would leave.

Beth begged for a length of green ribbon that they passed in a shop window and Louisa nodded, hard pressed to deny the girl anything. They found several pairs of gloves and a dozen yards of colored ribbons before they left the establishment. Mrs. Winslow uncovered a bolt of charcoal gray material that she purchased for a day dress. Exhilarated, they returned to their carriage and Beth entertained them with humorous *ondits* she imagined about the gentleman in the jeweler's.

Louisa knew her quiet mood would be remarked upon but found it hard to put her thoughts aside. She recollected her Aunt Louisa to be an extremely energetic woman who was always kind to her. *But how would she react to this charade?*

The medallion incident she put from her, feeling that it was an isolated event. Once it was learned that The Antiquarian Society had visited her, there would be no more said about it. Everyone would assume that she had given the medallion to the group. *Yet, how would she keep the Society from demanding that she produce the medallion before her aunt arrived?*

Mrs. Winslow held her aside for a moment as they entered the house and managed to express her concern over Louisa's early morning ride as well as their present situation. "After all, it is not only your own reputation at stake over this charade," she reminded her sternly. "It is mine and Beth's that will suffer if we are found out."

"I know and you are right, Jane. It will not happen again," Louisa assured her about the ride. "As to the medallion, I believe we should hear no more of it."

Mrs. Winslow was surprised and a little apprehensive that someone should take note of her suggestions. She left the Duchess at her chamber door and went to lie down and consider the possibilities.

Louisa had another scold from Betty who hadn't had the time earlier while she had been so busy putting on the heavy makeup to enable Louisa to become the dowager. But her words were succinct when she helped the Duchess from her gown and combed out her hair.

"Going out alone like a common—"

"Please, Betty, no more," Louisa begged. "I have apologized and told you it will not happen again. I would gladly write it in blood if it would reassure you and keep you from pulling my hair out as you comb it."

Betty sniffed and eased up her hold on the thick, pale hair. "I suppose you'll want those places touched up on your face?"

The Dowager Duchess

Louisa faced her in the mirror, the answer in her eyes. She promised herself, while Betty took out the face paint, that she wouldn't falter in her chosen role again. It was too dangerous to her plan.

Besides, now she had the extra complication of her aunt. Surely, even if she banished her from her house for impersonating her, she would take over as Beth's chaperone when she heard the tale? The most important thing was not to allow the masquerade to be revealed. It would humiliate her aunt as well.

Louisa could not let that happen. So, at least for the present, she would not go riding alone again in the morning. She would wear her bombazine and her makeup and play at being her aunt. Beth would be married and happy and she would have Osbourne Park to go back to when it was all over.

As she had predicted, Beth was a success. Flowers piled on tables and bureaus attested to that fact while invitations flowed like honey into the house between gifts. Two young gentlemen had already quarreled on the front walk before the ladies had come down for breakfast earlier that morning. Fleet had dismissed them.

A young man, Lord Cambridge, came to call with his high-perch black phaeton. Louisa watched as Beth stepped out into the sunshine with her pale green parasol matching her smart walking dress. The race was on!

"Good morning, Your Grace," Andrew called from the sidewalk, his eyes leaving Beth's slender form only with difficulty. "I trust the mad crush at the Marklands' rout left no lasting damage to you or Miss Montgomery?"

"Indeed, no, Lord Osbourne," Louisa said stiffly. "As you can see, my great niece is in perfect health this morning."

Indeed he could see it! Beth had smiled at him as she had climbed into the phaeton with Cambridge. Andrew had known an intense desire to throw himself under the wheels to keep them from going. Again he had been on his way to see the young lady and again, he had been thwarted!

It was absurd that he should find her so attractive. Especially since Miss Montgomery was closely related to the Duchess of Osbourne, his sworn enemy. "Will you be accompanying Miss Montgomery to the Hawthorns' ball tonight?"

"No." Louisa decided to see just how far the boy's infatuation went with her niece. "She will be making her debut at Almack's tonight." She could hear his quickly suppressed groan. Almack's was definitely not the place a young rake like Andrew would spend time. "Perhaps we shall see you there, my lord."

"Doubtful," he muttered to the air where the dowager had been.

Almack's! He had not been in years. None of his companions would be there except for George Benton perhaps, since his parents had told him to start setting up his nursery. Why the devil did every young, available Miss have to head posthaste for that straitlaced den of prudes? Not that he himself had enough experience with young Misses to fathom the answer. He had always preferred the Fashionable Impure. He had kept his own ladybird for the past year before Lord Thomas had got her away.

Miss Montgomery was exceptional, he decided, clamping his hat down firmly on his head. But nothing was worth the misery of Almack's!

Louisa had her tea slowly, trying not to feel bored and slightly out of charity with herself. At Osbourne she would have ridden out that day, worrying about the new crops growing and talking to the tenants.

Even the tasks of presiding over a house were denied to her. Aunt Louisa's house ran like clockwork. Her servants may have been used to infrequent usage of the townhouse but there was nothing slack in the management. The wood was polished to a shine and smelled of beeswax, the draperies were aired. Not so much as a cobweb graced any corner in the domicile. The food was excellent and the servants were quiet and efficient. She wouldn't dare think of interfering in their processes.

That left her sitting alone on a gorgeous day with nothing to do and makeup on her face. The stiff gown rustled around her when she moved. Bombazine was not the most comfortable of materials.

"Your Grace." Fleet bowed slightly. "A gentleman to see you. I have put him in the study."

"To see me?" Louisa asked, surprised. She took his card from the butler's gloved hand. *Lord Stanton*. A chill went up her spine. She stiffened her carriage, held her head up a little higher. "Very well."

Fleet bowed her into the front study. The window faced the street and it was there Lord Stanton waited, turning around as he heard her entrance. "Your Grace." Devon took her hand and bowed over it briefly. "I am—er—genuinely glad to see you. I trust you are well?"

"Indeed, thank you, Lord Stanton. To what do I owe the honor of your visit?" Was it her imagination or was there something of surprise to his manner?

"Actually, Your Grace, I had sent your man to ask your *niece* if she might want to drive in the park this afternoon."

"My niece?" Louisa was affronted. "Do you mean to court Elsbeth, my lord?"

"I am well and truly embarrassed, Your Grace." Devon managed to look shamefaced although his eyes twinkled madly.

"How so?" she demanded.

"I have come for the Duchess of Osbourne. After you told me that she was ill, I thought she might wish a drive to clear away the cobwebs. I am sorry if I was misunderstood."

"Of course." Louisa looked down at the pattern in the rug. "I also wish to apologize for my sharpness."

"Naturally someone must protect the young, Your Grace," he pointed out. "Is—er—the Duchess up from her sick bed?"

Thoughts scampered madly through her head, all to be rejected off hand. The day was made to be out of doors with the flowers and the blue sky. But she had made her decision when she had journeyed to London. "My niece has already left, Lord Stanton. She journeys to the Continent as we speak."

He appeared momentarily disconcerted, so certain had he been of his plan. After briefly considering a plan to follow Louisa to Osbourne, he had decided to press her into remaining in town. Their liaison would be so much easier here.

"Lord Stanton?"

"My apologies." He regained use of his brain and his tongue, disappointment sharpening the green of his eyes. "I am happy the Duchess is so much better. I thought I had understood that she traveled to Osbourne?"

Louisa blinked her eyes and then nodded her head. "Perhaps I misunderstood, my lord. Perhaps she does go to Osbourne."

He considered her strange words. "I am sorry if I have inconvenienced you, Your Grace."

"Not at all." She nodded graciously, wishing he would leave.

Indeed, he seemed inclined to do just that until he turned and looked up fiercely at the painting just above the fireplace. "You are very much alike," he remarked. "I know you find it boring, Your Grace, so I will not continue. Perhaps we shall see one another as you chaperone your great-niece."

"Perhaps," she agreed, hating to see the pained expression in his eyes. "And perhaps my niece and I are more alike than I like to admit, Lord Stanton. Louisa might have gained some of her dislike of town from me. I shall only be persuaded to be here until Beth has found a husband."

"Yes." He smiled and nodded vaguely, noticing for the first time a slight difference between the young duchess in the portrait on the wall and the Duchess of Osbourne. "Thank you for your time, Your Grace."

Louisa listened for his footsteps to echo into silence and watched for his coach to drive away.

"Your Grace?"

His voice startled her and she jumped back from the window. "Yes—uh—Lord Stanton?"

"Perhaps it is presumptuous of me—"

She tried to still her madly fluttering heart and face him serenely. "Yes?" She was at a loss. Had she missed something?

"Would you care to drive out with me? The day is so lovely and since I have missed your niece, I find myself with an afternoon that promises to be a boring waste ... unless I might have your company?"

She looked at him and knew that she would go even

while she told herself that she should not, must not. His eyes pleaded with hers and his smile was irresistible. What could a drive in the sunshine hurt so long as she was the dowager? She could even use the time to try and fathom what her next move should be and how to spin tales more convincingly in the future. She smiled at him. "I should be delighted, my lord."

The afternoon was pleasantly warm, the sun shining golden on everything from the trees to the open carriages. Their occupants laughed and called to one another. The traffic moved haltingly in the crush of drivers.

"I have heard a great deal of your exploits," Lord Stanton began as he helped her into his open carriage.

"Really?" Louisa refused to think about the warm touch of his hands on her waist. Did they linger for just a moment too long? Was he just a shade too close? She adjusted her veiled bonnet to shade her face from the sun. Too much heat would ruin her makeup.

"Indeed." He nodded, sitting beside her in the new rig. He took the reins from his tiger. "You are nearly famous. Your finds from Crete were exhibited here last year."

Louisa briefly recalled receiving a missive from her aunt last year, mentioning the exhibit. She felt fortunate to be able to recall even that much with him sitting so close to her. It had been years since she had ridden out with a man, not her father or a servant. What *was* the correct distance between them?

Friends hailed him as they entered the park. When he looked down at her and smiled, she thought she would faint with pleasure.

Get hold of yourself, she counseled fiercely, wondering, not for the first time what possessed her when she was with him. It was as though he was some Bacchanal sprite sent

The Dowager Duchess 101

to rob her of her senses. "I have heard of your exploits as well," Louisa returned the compliment. "You are quite famous from what my niece has told me."

He looked at her strangely. Indeed, intent to the point of rudeness. Then he glanced away. When he looked back, the easy smile was in place. "Ah yes, the Duchess of Osbourne. I am certain she has had little good to say about me."

"She has merely mentioned your work for the government during the war. You have been quite an infamous spy, I suspect." He was studying her mouth. It wasn't her imagination. She feigned a sudden interest in the floral display, red tulips surrounded by golden yellow daffodils.

"Your niece, I'm afraid, doesn't see me in the same golden light as you do, Your Grace. I am surprised that she would mention my working for the war effort. I'm not certain what I have done to make her have a dislike of me."

"She doesn't dislike you," she hastened to reassure him. "I'm sure she finds you . . . quite admirable."

He sighed. "I had been hoping for some warmer feelings from her. Perhaps you might speak with her on my behalf, Your Grace."

Louisa wished she could put her hands to her head in frustration. Now, he would have her talking to herself to gain her own approval! It was ridiculous! She had to put an end to his quest of her! "Louisa will never marry, my lord. She is quite happy with her life as it is."

"That does not surprise me. I recall hearing that she hastened her father's death when the will was drawn up so that she might have Osbourne for herself."

"What?" She rounded on him furiously, nearly forgetting herself. "Louisa would never . . . her father wanted her to have the estate . . . there was no one else!"

"It was only a rumor, Your Grace," he said quickly, the carriage coming to a standstill in the traffic.

She stared at him for an instant, feeling the danger emanating from his clear eyes hidden by the dark fringe of his lashes. Being the object of that sharply probing gaze made her feel a great deal like a butterfly caught on a pin to be dissected at his will.

"I feel I should return, my lord," she addressed him calmly. "I find I grow fatigued quite easily of late." There was a brief moment when she thought he was going to insist that she reply to his statement. She held her breath and did not dare draw another until he smiled and she knew that he had relented.

"Of course, Your Grace," he answered lightly. "I do apologize for wearing you out. I had not thought you would be taxed by such a brief outing after all your years on the sites in Greece."

"I have not been well, but I am recovering now that I am home again," she responded quietly.

"I share that feeling." He sighed. "I have been like a ghost haunting the night-time streets. Too long, I think sometimes, in the company of war and fear."

They were silent until they reached the townhouse door. Fleet discreetly stood to the side, seen and yet unseen.

"I want to thank you for your company, Your Grace." He bowed over her gloved hand. "You took pity on me, did you not?"

She smiled at him, her eyes carefully on his face. She was terribly conscious of the fact that he still held her hand in his own. "It is a lovely day, my lord. Too much so to spend it alone. For either of us, I think."

"You are as gracious as you are beautiful," he rejoined.

"And you are either blind or a terrible liar, Lord Stanton." Louisa laughed.

"Call me Devon, please."

She retrieved her hand from his and looked away. "I must go. Thank you for the outing."

"We shall doubtless see each other in passing," he reminded her.

"Doubtless," she agreed. "Good day, Lord Stanton."

She stepped into the townhouse and Fleet closed the door quietly behind her. She stood for a moment with her eyes closed.

"Are you all right, Your Grace?" Fleet inquired briefly.

"Fine," she answered, lying with a smile. In just a few days, Lord Stanton had taken her calm, ordered existence and turned her life upside down. Whatever would she do?

Almack's was glittering. The night outside was dark and threatening rain, but inside the hallowed walls, laughter rang out. Discreetly, of course. Music played and ladies flirted with gentlemen who smiled, their eyes promising what their actions could not. Whispers and heated glances added spice to the dances.

The Princess Lieven watched as the dancers swirled by in the waltz, the dance she had introduced just a short while before. Careful scrutiny was given to the space between the dancers' bodies, noting the heads that were bent too closely or the hands that strayed.

When the Princess saw the dowager enter the rooms with her radiant young niece at her side, she took her leave of the lady beside her and made a short pathway to the Duchess' side. "Louisa!" she greeted her friend, diamonds sparkling in her hair and around her throat. "I am so happy to see you have come! Let us have some punch while the youngsters find their way."

Miss Watson, Colonel Parker's niece, claimed Beth at once and the two went away giggling.

Louisa was unsettled. She was uneasy, even though she knew she looked perfectly costumed in her face paint and her midnight blue gown. But she was not emotionally prepared for the masquerade that night.

Her ride with Lord Stanton that afternoon had disturbed her more than she was willing to credit. There had been something about the expression on his face when he had looked at her in the park. It had made her doubt the wisdom of her actions, even though her path was clearly laid out before her.

It was possibly the news regarding her aunt that had thrown her whole world out of joint. She was torn between wanting to go home and staying with Beth in London; between wanting to escape to what had been her safe haven for four years and bearding the lions in their den.

As she moved about the *ton* with confidence, inwardly she was terrified that she would be found out. The implications of such a thing left her weak-kneed when she stopped to consider it. What had she got herself into? Yet what choice had she had when it came to Beth's only chance for happiness?

As for Lord Stanton, there was no doubt that he should have found Louisa's quick leave-taking a direct cut. Yet still he attempted to enlist the dowager's aid in speaking with her. She walked to the punch bowl with the Princess chattering beside her, filling her in on the latest gossip. She could not be involved with Lord Stanton, she reminded herself. Her life was her own, but she would lose everything she had worked for with a sweep of his hand.

The Dowager Duchess

Young men and women surrounded Beth at her place in the heart of the room. When the first dance was started, she was whirled away by a young man Louisa didn't recognize.

"Lord Renders," the Princess supplied seeing the dowager's glance. "Relax, Louisa, dear. Renders is of the best stock. He will be an Earl someday. Remember, she is as safe here as in her own home. We have a reputation here. The young men we admit to Almack's keep their place."

Louisa sat beside the Princess in the straight-back chairs, watching the dancing, wishing, despite herself, that she were twirling across the floor. *Not with Lord Stanton.* She amended her mental image of him as her partner. The man was too often in her thoughts!

Beth did not yet have permission to waltz but that did not seem to hamper her steady stream of partners. Her daffodil yellow gown was pale beside the black formal coat of Lord Cambridge as they danced. She was laughing at something he had said, smiling up into his face.

"She is lovely, Your Grace."

She was startled but managed to keep from jumping up. She barely turned her head to glance at him. "Lord Stanton! I fancy this to be a surprise to all."

"Indeed, ma'am," he agreed, taking the seat recently vacated by the Princess when she had spotted a possible indiscretion. "None so surprised as myself."

She looked at him, studying the line of his profile as he watched the dancers across the room. "Looking for a wife, my lord?"

He laughed and turned to her. "Is that what everyone is doing here tonight?"

"I believe some are," she replied, feeling nervous and uneasy.

"Your great-niece is doing her part, Your Grace. I believe most of the young men in the room are accommodating her."

Louisa saw Andrew, splendidly handsome in his intricate cravat, the diamond stickpin in the snowy white cloth winking in the light. He made his bow before Beth and took her hand, leading her on to the floor. Louisa did not realize how angry she was until she felt her hand gripping the black cane tightly.

"You do not like to see your great-niece with Andrew?"

He saw too much, she realized, losing her white-knuckled hold on the cane. "I believe the young man to be an unsavory influence in my niece's life. Can you think else wise?"

"I would not deny it." He shook his head slowly. "Andrew is impulsive and possesses poor judgment in many cases. However, he is young and he will grow into his station."

"As you did, my lord?"

"As I did, Your Grace. As we all did, did we not?" He smiled at her, his eyes very direct on her face.

"Why are you not dancing?" she demanded huskily, turning her face away. He was studying her again, as was his usual disconcerting habit. "There must be many young ladies that would be happy of your attention."

"There is only one I am interested in attending, Your Grace. As you told me earlier, she has retired to the country. Or France." He looked down at his hands then returned his gaze to her face. "Perhaps you could tell me why?"

"I would like very much to be of assistance to you, my lord." She kept her tone even though her heart was racing. "But I am not certain I know the answer."

"I do not mean to pry." He shrugged his broad shoulders. "Well, perhaps I do."

"I—I am certain you should ask her. Gossip is so unsavory, is it not?"

He weathered her intent stare and smiled quickly, looking back towards the dancers. "Unsavory? Perhaps."

"Indeed." The Duchess raised her chin a trifle higher, straightened her back a little straighter. "If there was something she wanted you to know, I am certain she would have told you. But suffice it to say, she is not the marrying kind."

"Thank you, Your Grace."

She searched the room for Beth's pale yellow gown and found her, dancing with yet another young gentleman.

"I am about to throw myself at your mercy," he confessed, watching the dancers on the highly polished floor. "I can see no other way."

"What are you saying, my lord?"

He bowed his head. The light glinted on the bright strands in his hair. "I am infatuated with your niece, Louisa."

That was unexpected. If she had thought that her direct cut would chase him away, she was apparently mistaken.

"W-what is it that you believe I can do for you, Lord Stanton?"

"Please, call me Devon."

She nodded. "If you will call me Louisa."

He looked back at her. "Was she named for you, Louisa? Were you close to her parents?"

Louisa was nearly speechless. Her brain was functioning but it didn't want to find answers to these questions.

"Please," he asked of her, taking her hand in his where it lay on her lap. "Whatever you can impart could help me."

Heat immediately suffused Louisa's entire body. She wished that she had brought a fan instead of a cane! "I—uh—yes. I was close to her mother."

"What of Louisa's mother?"

"Yes. Certainly. She—uh—had a mother," Louisa replied, still so conscious of his touch that she could barely speak. "It is very warm in here. Hard to breathe."

At once, he was all concern. He took her hand and helped her to her feet. "Let me assist you! We shall take a turn in the garden for some air."

Chapter Seven

Louisa didn't think it was a good idea to go out into the garden, alone, with him. In her guise as the dowager, she was beyond reproach and certainly beyond the rules that fit for younger members of Society. Yet, that didn't change him being close against her side to support her. Or her hand tucked into his arm. He was smiling and talking to her as they stepped out into the cooler night air.

"The room was close," he said as they started down the path that led through the tiny garden. "This is much better."

"You are so helpful," she murmured.

"Devon," he encouraged her to use his name.

"Devon," she replied carefully.

"I didn't mean to shock you with my request," he apologized. "Just that your niece is unapproachable."

Louisa marshaled her thoughts. "I shall not help you seduce my niece, Devon. She has decided her own fate."

He stopped walking and looked at her. "In this light, you could be her."

She looked up at him. Her heart pounded in her throat. At that moment, she would have given anything to throw off her disguise. She would have given anything to feel his lips on hers. All she could do was swallow hard and look away. She reminded herself of Beth's future and her own. She could not tell him her secret.

She laughed. It sounded hollow in the quiet of the garden but it broke the mood between them. "You can't hope to charm me with your winning ways, Devon! What is it you want from me?"

"Only your counsel, gentle lady," he answered. "How shall I find Louisa? Where has she gone?"

Louisa considered his handsome face in the pale light. "You are truly enamored of her?"

He nodded. "I believe she has feelings for me as well, Louisa. I am only asking for the chance to see her, talk to her. Then she can make her own choice."

She took her hand from his and started back towards the ballroom. "That is impossible."

"Why?" he questioned.

"Because Louisa is happy alone."

"No one is happy alone," he argued. "She's still young. You can't want that for her."

"It is what she wants for herself," she continued fiercely. She turned abruptly and faced him. "She would tell you herself—"

"That," he cut her off, "is all I am asking for. A short meeting. If I tell her my feelings and she does want to be alone, I would leave her so."

"Truly?" Louisa challenged him. "She did tell me that

she thought you would leave her alone after your last meeting. Yet, here you are, once again, pleading with me."

"Louisa?" Colonel Parker called her name.

She started to reply, glad to escape the heated debate.

Devon took her hand. "Set a time and place of her choosing. If she tells me then that she has no use for me, I shall not attempt to see her again. You have my word."

Louisa knew it was risky. She was determined to see out her charade to help her niece. But she was very attracted to him. Was her determination strong enough to see her through a tête-à-tête with him? She could feel herself weakening in her resolve not to see him again as herself. How could she hope to hold out against him in that face of that emotional onslaught?

"Louisa?" Colonel Parker called again in his raspy voice. "Are you all right, m'dear?"

· "I have to go," she said to Devon.

"Promise me the meeting, Louisa. Promise me you'll convince her."

"All right," she promised breathlessly. "I shall speak to her. But I make no promises of her response."

"That is all I ask." He brought her hand quickly to his mouth and kissed it. Then he escorted her back to the ballroom.

Colonel Parker was obviously put out by finding the two of them alone in the garden. He was solicitous when Louisa explained that she had felt faint. He went gladly to procure her a glass of ratafia though he gave Lord Stanton a withering glance as he left them.

"I shall take my leave of you now," Lord Stanton said, helping her find a chair. He took her gloved hand. "I hope your niece is a smashing success."

"Yes, thank you," she replied coolly, glad that he was leaving finally. "And what shall I hope for you, my lord?"

The candlelight shone on the golden streaks in his hair. He smiled. "I wish only for those things other men long for, Your Grace. And the keeping of your promise to me. You may wish any or all of those things for me. And for yourself?"

Louisa managed a humphing sound and stamped her cane. "I am past the age of wishing for anything but a good meal and an early bed. But I shall keep my promise, Lord Stanton."

She watched him walk away, weaving his way through the crowd until he came to where her niece sat, surrounded by her friends. He brought Sally Jersey with him from a nearby group. As Louisa watched, the patroness nodded and Lord Stanton led Beth out on the floor for her first waltz.

For just an instant, Louisa's eyes met Devon's across the room filled with people, and for that time, it was as though they were the only ones present.

Then the dance took Devon away and Louisa was left there, watching Andrew's angry face as he glowered from the side of the room.

Of course, she would not meet him! It was preposterous! She lay in her bed later that evening. She could not sleep but was staring up at the dark ceiling.

After Lord Stanton had left her at Almack's, Colonel Parker had joined her, talking with her late into the evening. The man was evidently infatuated with her aunt and had wanted to push their relationship further now they were both in town again. He sat a little too close, talked a great deal too much. He described in long drawling tones his house and land in Surrey, the horses he raced, the dreams he had for the future. A future he envisioned as being shared by the two of them.

Dorothea Lieven and Lady Celeste Townsend visited her at one time or another that evening. They had talked about old times, some of which Louisa had heard her aunt talk about. Some she had to nod and laugh to gloss over.

She had fooled them all, including Lord Stanton. So, why did she feel so restless and unhappy? Louisa decided long after all other sounds in the house were silent that she might as well be about. She would not sleep that night, trying to decide which was the least of the two evils.

If she met with Lord Stanton, she would have the opportunity to tell him that she never wanted to see him again. If he kept his word, he would stay away from her forever. But if she agreed to meet with him and he seduced her, it would mean the end to it all. She wandered the corridors of the townhouse like a wraith while the other occupants of the house slept around her. Except for the little kitchen boy who was up early, preparing for the coming day.

The sky was turning gray outside when she reached the study where her Aunt Louisa's picture hung. She sat down on the green brocade sofa and looked up at the face so like her own. "What would you do?"

Aunt Louisa was very practical. She would say that Devon couldn't find her as long as she was disguised as someone else. There was no reason that she couldn't tell him that Louisa had refused a meeting with him.

It was her traitorous mind that went blank at his touch that wanted to hear what he had to say to her. It was her lips that craved one perfect kiss from him, the one that had been interrupted in the library at Osbourne. And it was her heart that was eager to fall in love with this handsome, vibrant man.

The first downstairs maid came into the study later that morning to clean and found the Duchess asleep on the sofa. Not certain what to do in such a position, she called for the first footman who was baffled as well. He did assure the maid that he would handle the problem and that she should go on to another room.

Quietly, he revealed their predicament to Fleet, as he was taking the delivery of a huge spray of roses for the Duchess from Colonel Parker's servant. Fleet, having served the Rothner family since he was a young child, sent the footman on his way. He took two more invitations and another floral design at the door and then made his way to Her Grace's maid's room where he made known to her where the Duchess was at present.

So it was to Betty's anxious face that Louisa awoke, her head pounding. Her eyes felt like grit was rubbed into them. "What? Betty, where—?"

"Let me help you up to your room, Your Grace." Betty took her arm, wrapping the faded pink wrapper closer around her Lady's frame.

"What time is it? Oh, Betty, I must go."

"Go? Where would you go this early? You look ill to me. You need to get into bed and let us send for the doctor. You are obviously not well," Betty fussed.

Louisa pulled away from the maid and took possession of her own wrap. "I can go by myself, Betty. I am not an invalid."

"Of course you're not," Betty soothed her. "I was just helping you."

Louisa lay down on her bed when she reached her room,

intending to lie down only for a moment for her head to stop pounding.

When Betty returned with her usual cup of chocolate, she was already fast asleep. The maid tsked and left her there, pulling the heavy draperies against the sun. She informed Beth and the rest of the household that the Duchess was ill.

For two days, Louisa cowered there beneath the quilts. The first day she had truly felt ill. The doctor had come and gone. Louisa refused to see him, then had alternately slept and stared at the ceiling, feeling hot and nauseous.

The second day, she was merely lacking enough spirit to get out of her bed and face what had happened to her. She saw no one but Betty and ate very little, sleeping between bouts of remorse and wondering what she was going to do. But to her ultimate consternation, her mind had begun to function again. She tried to quash her thoughts but they poured through.

It wasn't like her. She had not cowered after her father's death when the relatives had scorned her inheritance and threatened to take it from her. She had faced them outright. All their wailing about fair play and male heirs had merely strengthened her determination to have what was hers.

Beth's involvement was what made this so much worse. But it wasn't her love for Beth that finally put resolve in her backbone on the morning of the third day.

It was so early the sky was barely light. No one was astir when Louisa made her way down the stairs in a dark blue riding habit. Her matching hat cast shadows on her face as she rounded the corner to the door. She had sent word to Lord Stanton that she'd agreed to meet with him, and knew he would be waiting. She pulled on her gloves, squared her chin, and walked briskly out into the morning.

The air was heavy with the promise of rain. The city moved sleepily as though the fog in the streets clouded more than the debris. The stable boy, no older than ten, held the mare's reins as she mounted. She thanked him quietly. The horse's hooves echoed in the fog as Louisa guided her towards the paths in the park.

Mist hid the tops of the trees and swirled along the ground, making Louisa feel as though she were alone in the world. There were only the sounds of a few birds and the horse's quiet plodding as they followed the same path they'd followed before.

Louisa knew he was there a moment before her horse snorted and she heard his horse coming along the ground. She waited, knowing running would do no good. There was nowhere far enough to run to hide from herself.

"I knew you would come," he said, appearing through the fog.

"I was at Osbourne," she lied. "Or I should have been here sooner."

He dismounted smoothly, tying his horse to a nearby tree branch then walked over to where she still sat on the mare. "Come down, Louisa. We shall be able to talk better without the beasts, I think."

She was hesitant for an instant, almost considering the possibility of flight. Looking at him, knowing that he was going to touch her, weakened her resolve. She knew what she had to do. There was one thing she had promised herself before she never saw him again as Louisa Drayton.

"I shall not murder you here amidst the fog, Your Grace," he said tentatively, seeing the hunted look in her face. "Let me help you down."

She had, it seemed, little choice. He put his hands to her waist and lowered her down to the ground. They were almost of a height. Both were tall. He, broad shouldered and slim hipped. She, softly curved with long legs and graceful gloved hands that she placed hesitantly on his shoulders.

Louisa could feel her heart beating a little faster. Breathless anticipation that was both frightening and exhilarating raced through her treacherous, hateful body. She told herself that it disgusted her. Her pupils dilated as his mouth hovered so close to her own. She passed from panic to anticipation to disappointment in an instant. She was relieved, she told herself scornfully, when he did not press her.

He watched her face as she lowered her eyes from his and stepped back, drawing her hands from his shoulders. Slowly, almost painfully, he moved his own hands from her waist.

She waited while he tied her mount to the branch near them.

"You needn't look as though you are facing your last moments on earth," he said, taking her arm as they started to walk along the soft, damp ground.

She raised her head, wanting to jerk her arm away from his grasp but staying at his side. "Can you blame me for being . . . apprehensive?"

"Have I done something that would make you so? I only requested your presence here to allow us time to converse." His smile was warm on her face, but his eyes watched her carefully.

She did tear her arm away from him at that moment, facing him with angry eyes. "I thought I had already made it clear to you that there can be nothing between us."

He kept his smile. "I know."

"Then why are we here?" she demanded in great agitation.

"Because of this," he said quietly and took her in his arms.

He kissed her. Not the one chaste kiss that she had promised herself she would have before she left him that morning; not the innocent promise that would never be fulfilled. His kisses were long and slow. Soft as a butterfly wing, gentle as a faint spring breeze. Before she could protest, the words were swept from her mind by their seduction. She had pictured herself as lying quiescent in his arms while his lips touched hers.

Instead, there was a slow build-up of energy that ignited in her. It turned her limbs to pudding and scrambled her brain. The want of him exploded in her, swamping her reason and her logic. It made her forget everything but that need that burned through her. The need to touch and be touched.

When he released her, she looked at him through a haze of desire. She wanted to cry out at the loss of his arms around her. She put a hand up to her kiss-swollen lips.

He was not unmoved by the intimate caress. His breath came a little faster and the hands that still held hers, trembled slightly. His eyes were so green. A lock of his hair had fallen forward and she reached to move it back

He waited as she touched him then took her hand back in his and kissed the palm, his lips lingering on her sweetness. "I knew it would be this way between us," he told her quietly. "I could see it in your beautiful eyes."

A bird flew up from the bushes nearby and Louisa thought she felt the first droplets of rain. She took her hands from his and turned away from him. "What do you want from me?"

"Want?" He stopped smiling and his eyes became intent. "I want only your happiness."

"Surely you see that this cannot be."

He turned her back to face him. "No. I do not see anything of the sort, Louisa. Why can't this happen?"

"I have learned about Society, Devon." She used his name easily. "I cannot meet you in some place you set up for our trysts without losing everything. My relations wait like vultures for me to make that mistake. And I am not such a country bumpkin as to believe that you offer marriage."

His eyes were rapiers on her face. "I see you have thought everything through. How careless of me to have thought that love would find a way."

She smiled. "You would survive that love and go on to find another. I would be left homeless and alone, without so much as a farthing to my name."

"Is that what this is all about?" he demanded. "If so, I am willing to pay very well for your services, Your Grace."

"You mock me!" she declared. "But you know as well as I that it is true. Men go unscathed by their affairs. Women are marked forever."

He shook his head. "I know only that I have been lost in your eyes since I met you, Louisa." He touched the side of her face with a gentle hand. "I feel as though I have wanted you forever. How can you be so quick to judge me?"

Every fiber in her wanted to lean her head against his hand, to touch him and feel his lips on hers again. But with what little will power she had to resist him, she shook her head. "Please, do not try to see me again. Do not enlist my aunt against me. Find another."

"You don't mean that!"

"I do," she repeated. "I agreed to meet with you. You agreed to leave me in peace."

"Louisa!" He made to reach for her and she turned from him. Moving with the speed and agility of a practiced rider, she mounted her horse and fled down the path she had come. She didn't look back.

He would have followed her but for her last statement. If she had shown any sign that she might relent, he would have gone after her. But her words had been very clear, very certain of his position. And, in good faith, she was right. He had not thought of marriage. He had also not thought of ruining her. Liaisons were common between ladies and gentlemen of the *ton*. She wasn't a young girl. Her family must indeed be vultures if they would not turn a blind eye.

She meant to live out her life alone, he considered, mounting his own horse. He had given his word that he would let her go.

The next few days passed uneventfully after Louisa had endured Betty's scolds that morning. Why had she gone riding again? Did she want to be found out and ruin her life?

Mrs. Winslow had not mentioned the event but her silence and chill manner were eloquent. Only Beth seemed unconcerned about Louisa's ride in the park. She chatted happily about the parties they had attended, the people she had met. Mrs. Winslow and Louisa played with the breakfast they had been served while Beth ate up every bite.

The remainder of Beth's new dresses had arrived along with several impassioned pleas from gentlemen who wanted to court her. Beth laughed them away, saying they were not what she wanted . . . unless Aunt Louisa considered them necessary?

Louisa did not and said so. "When the right young man comes along, you will know, my dearest. Until then, the rest are to be part of the experience." However, she did take the precaution of having Mr. Reresby check into the young men's backgrounds. Beth was not an heiress. Louisa had pledged her a dowry, however, and there could be some unscrupulous men out there who would be willing to take whatever she could give.

Beth could have told her aunt that she had already found the right young man but knew it was not yet the right time. Aunt Louisa was determined that she should not be involved with Andrew. It would take time to change her mind. Besides, that certain young man had not been one of those to suggest marriage. He was always there, waiting to dance with her, seemingly interested in her, but the words were not forthcoming. Beth hoped he would not wait too long.

In the afternoon, they went to a picnic sponsored by Lady Townsend for a large group of young people as well as most of Louisa's contemporaries. The weather, which had been foggy and filled with the promise of rain, cleared away and the picnic went as proposed in the Townsends' beautifully sculpted yard.

The pale muslin gowns worn by the young ladies dotted the green grass like large flowers. White tablecloths were placed about the grass, covered with huge amounts of food that was served by red-liveried servants. Laughter floated through the trees along with the breeze. Louisa watched as Beth sat on a white cloth, her pink and green striped gown spread around her. Several young men were urging her to eat from their plates, Andrew among them.

Louisa did not like to see them together but was careful not to urge Beth away from him, for that would surely cause more interest than Andrew warranted. She would lean towards Beth's natural good sense and if that failed, she would simply warn the young man away.

Louisa was relieved to see that Lord Stanton had not been invited to the picnic. Clarisse Townsend was overheard telling Sally Jersey that she would not have invited the so handsome Stanton. He was much too debauched to appreciate the virtues of a yard full of young ladies. Though *she* was not too debauched to appreciate *his* virtues. Laughter followed among the ladies and a few carefully chosen remarks about that gentleman's attributes. A prodigious amount of fans were brought forth to cool suddenly warm faces.

Louisa toyed with her food, trying not to think about Devon. To hear others discuss him was like a sword to her heart. There was idle speculation that he might marry and start a family now that he was back from the war. Although most of the ladies agreed 'twould be a waste. Lord Stanton was so handsome, so elegant. Such a devil with the ladies, with his green eyes and his sun-lightened hair, his fine turn of leg and muscular shoulders.

With a deep sigh, she left them, murmuring an excuse about finding Beth and having a headache.

She found the girl, alone with Andrew, walking through a grove of poplars away from the rest of the group. Both their faces were troubled. They looked as though they had been kissing. She held her tongue and explained to Beth that she needed to leave the picnic.

Beth surprised her by being only too happy to oblige. She sat opposite her in the carriage, gazing soulfully out the window.

"Is something wrong, dearest?"

"No, Aunt. Nothing is wrong. What could be wrong?"

"Did you not enjoy the picnic?" Louisa wondered.

"I did enjoy it. Thank you for taking me. I am not myself today."

"Dearest," Louisa began, trying to be subtle.

"You do not have to tell me that Andrew is all wrong for me," Beth forestalled her. "I have found that out on my own."

"There are many others."

"I know, Aunt Louisa." She wiped a tear from the corner of one eye. "I know."

Louisa sighed heavily. "Life and love are not always easy, dearest. Sometimes we may want something so much that we cannot see that it is bad for us."

Beth looked at her with misty eyes. "Like you and Lord Stanton?"

Mrs. Winslow took in a sharp breath and looked askance at the Duchess. Louisa looked away. "It is not attractive for a young lady to be too outspoken," Mrs. Winslow gently corrected Beth in the absence of a response from Her Grace.

"I am sorry," Beth said, studying her hands. "It will not occur again."

Mrs. Winslow sat back on the scat, satisfied with her rebuke of the younger woman's curiosity. Then she proceeded to worry about the older woman's silence.

The three women stayed home that evening, surrounded by a general aura of malaise. There were barely a dozen words spoken between them as they ate dinner and played cards until bedtime.

Louisa knocked on Beth's bedroom door when she was certain Mrs. Winslow was tucked up in her bed with her chocolates. When Beth told her to enter, she closed the door quietly behind her and went to sit on the edge of her niece's bed.

"You looked so unhappy tonight, Beth," Louisa observed. "Is there no one you can find to suit you amongst all these handsome, young gentlemen?"

"I do not want you to think that I am ungrateful Aunt Louisa," Beth replied quietly. "But perhaps my Mama was right. Perhaps I should go home and marry the Viscount."

Louisa was shocked. "How can you say so? Even Andrew is better than that vile, old lecher."

"A husband can be a sight older than you," Beth answered pertly. "And the Marquess is no longer in question."

Louisa hugged her niece to her. "But there are still others! Tomorrow, we shall go out and start again! We shall buy a new dress and go to the opera where you will no doubt dazzle every young man who sees you!"

Beth cried a little into her aunt's pink wrapper. "How did I become so fortunate to have you as my aunt?"

"Because we were both so fortunate as to share your father," Louisa told her, tears flowing down her face. "Pray God that he is still alive."

"You know." Beth apprised her aunt through watery eyes. "When you aren't the dowager, you are so beautiful. I cannot believe that Lord Stanton—"

"Shush!" Louisa scolded her. "Didn't Mrs. Winslow make her position on Young Ladies Being Outspoken quite clear to you?"

Beth smiled and Louisa laughed and wiped her tears. "There! See, we are out of the doldrums now. These men shall not cut up our peace again."

"I love you, Aunt. You are too good to me."

"I love you, too, dearest child. Nothing is too good for you."

* * *

Beth and Louisa went to the opera the following evening, utilizing the dowager's rarely used box.

Maria Cassell was singing that night in Mozart's *Magic Flute*, drawing a huge crowd. La Cassell had not been in London for some time due to the war and everyone flocked there to see her.

Among the luckier ones of the peerage that had boxes, the crush was not so awful. On the floor, hundreds were pushed forward, packed in tightly until their colorful dresses and bright coats blended together. Their voices were loud with anticipation and too much wine. Several of the box holders recalled their feeling that the rabble should have been excluded from that particular performance since it had been rumored that Wellington might attend. Even though the rumor had been false, the Ladies of the *ton* as well as their counterparts, the Fashionable Impure, could not enjoy the performance for watching for him.

In the upper strata, jeweled bosoms heaved and glittering tiaras blazed in the light. Ladies in other boxes inspected dazzling dresses that cost the earth. Lady Dimity was scandalized to find that her dress had been copied for Lady Brightworthy, even down to the shade of blue that perfectly complemented their eyes, or so they had both been told.

Louisa was looking out into the melee when the curtain moved to admit Andrew Drayton and Lord Devon Stanton in the box almost across from them. Two more gentlemen, one of whom Louisa recognized as Sir Lawrence Chatham, accompanied them.

The women with them were of obvious disrepute. They laughed loudly and clung to them like gauze. There was no mistaking the lithe young woman in the daring red dress as the same female from the dress shop. Her hands, Louisa noted, were on Sir Lawrence, but her slightly slanted eyes were on Lord Stanton. Her gaze was decidedly feline.

Lord Stanton, as though feeling Louisa's gaze, looked directly towards her box. Louisa looked away rapidly. Her heart beat a terrible tattoo that made her put her hand to her breast as though to still it.

Devon smiled, a glint in his eye, half listening to Andrew as he extolled the virtues of golden-haired females.

Beth had already looked away and Louisa sighed, thankful that Andrew was definitely out of the running for her niece's affections. She didn't know what had happened between them but she did know that it could only be a blessing.

At that moment, their guests, Colonel Parker and his niece, Miss Annabelle Watson entered the box. The greetings exchanged were just in time for the performance to begin, the Colonel seated beside Louisa and Annabelle beside Beth.

"Quite a crowd," the Colonel said gruffly, looking around as the lights went down. He straightened his already mangled cravat and ran a hand through his thick white hair.

Louisa agreed silently. The Colonel, however, was not a silent partner. He continued to speak throughout the first act even though Louisa pointedly disregarded him. What was wrong with the man?

Several of their nearest neighbors shushed him. She heard the girls giggle behind them and sat up a trifle straighter in her chair. The theatre was dark but she could feel Lord Stanton's eyes upon her. It was only fancy, of course, she told herself. He would not be staring rudely at the dowager.

In the interim between acts, Louisa was glad when the

Colonel insisted on going for refreshments. The girls went with him, leaving her alone and in peace for the moment.

She was irritated to think she had heard barely any of the arias. In future, she would not invite the Colonel to anything for which listening was necessary. It was possible that the man could not hear well himself, she considered charitably, and therefore tried to make up by speaking constantly. While it was not so terrible in a crowded room, conversation buzzing around them in a theatre, it was too much.

"Good evening, Your Grace."

Her breath caught in her throat, strangling any other thought from her mind. She felt a blush work its way up her face. "Lord Stanton," she acknowledged. "I trust you are enjoying the performance?"

He smiled, sitting freely beside her. "Devon, please, Louisa."

"Devon," she repeated. "I have done as you asked, my lord. Are you prepared to keep your side of the bargain?"

"I am," he replied smoothly. "I but stopped by to thank you for your part in the bargain."

"I am sorry the matter did not end to your liking," she conceded, conscious of the black bombazine that she wore and the white powder in her hair. The face paint felt greasy and odious on her cheeks and neck.

He held her gaze with his own steady one. "Nonetheless, you have played your part beautifully."

"I—thank you, my lord." Just being near him generated enough heat in her body that she was worried about her make-up running!

He reached forward suddenly and took the diamond pendant that she wore around her neck in his long fingers. A ghost of satisfaction flirted in his eyes when she jumped back.

"You should be more careful, Louisa," he warned, his voice very low and his face suddenly very close. "Some would know this to be part of the Osbourne collection. It is unlikely your aunt would be wearing it."

"W-what are you saying?" she demanded breathlessly, still held to him by the gold chain.

"I know the truth, Your Grace."

Chapter Eight

She opened her mouth to ask him to release her even as the chain was drawing her inexorably closer to him. Her throat was dry and her eyes were panicked. He was going to kiss her! Short of making a scene, there was nothing she could do.

"Stanton!" Colonel Parker greeted him as he and the girls returned to the box.

"Colonel," Devon acknowledged him as he turned from Louisa's startled face, getting to his feet as he released her. He stayed between the Colonel and Louisa as he greeted the older man.

Louisa was grateful for his not moving immediately, giving her time to compose herself before she faced the girls and their new escort, Lord Cambridge. Quickly, she put the diamond pendant inside her black gown, high necked and long sleeved, covering it over for good measure with her black shawl.

Colonel Parker handed Louisa a glass of wine as he spoke with Stanton about the performance. It was amazing how knowledgeable he was about the music when he had talked throughout!

"Your Grace." Lord Cambridge made his bow over her hand. "I trust you are feeling well?"

"Indeed," she answered briefly, holding tightly to her black cane, wanting to swat Stanton with it. Betty was right. The man would be the ruin of her and yet she seemed helpless to avoid him. He said that he knew the truth. But what truth?

She had managed to fool everyone else. She wouldn't leap to the conclusion that he knew about her impersonation. It was probably something quite different and trivial to which he referred. Yet her pulse was leaping and her heart was pounding in her chest.

The lights began to lower when the gentlemen took their leave. The girls were excited and difficult to settle down. The Colonel was excited as well, it seemed, and he continued to talk randomly as he had before. Louisa gave up trying to hear the music but kept her eyes on the stage, her mind on the problem of Lord Stanton.

Had he really gained knowledge of her charade? There was that look in his eyes when he remarked that her aunt would be unlikely to wear an Osbourne diamond. It made her shudder to think such knowledge might be possible. And if he knew, would he give her away?

The knowledge could be used to blackmail her, she realized. He had seemed sincere when he told her that he wanted her. Louisa was not so innocent that she did not know what he could demand from her. And she was not so lacking in imagination that she could not imagine enjoying it. She remembered the feel of his lips on her own and shivered at the thought of those things she did not know.

The opera was finally over, the evening ruined, as far as Louisa was concerned.

Beth and Louisa waited with Colonel Parker and his niece, and Lord and Lady Townsend, while their carriage was brought up and the crowd cleared. Lord Cambridge danced attendance on the two girls who were obviously pleased to have him there. Lord Renders joined them after a few moments and Louisa listened to their conversation while she stood with the older group.

She half wondered what had become of Andrew as she had seen him with Devon earlier. But she could only be glad that he had left without taking up any of Beth's time. Lord Cambridge and Lord Renders were both fine young men, she thought, pleased that they were interested in Beth. Louisa smiled at her niece. Beth's gown was as blue as her eyes. Her blond hair was artfully curled around her animated young face.

If that young lady's gaze wandered occasionally from the group she stood with, Beth could only hope her aunt would fail to discern it.

When their carriage was brought round, they said their good-byes to the group and started out into the night. The crowd still milled loudly around the theatre steps. The smell of wine and smoke was strong in the thick night air. The bombazine rustled loudly as Louisa moved down the stairs. Beth was just behind her when a dark figure ran forward through the crowd. A rough hand pushed the girl out of the way and she fell back on the stairs with a tiny cry that alerted Louisa.

Lord Stanton, standing at his coach in the street, looked up as the man grabbed at Louisa, dragging her with him down the stairs. His arm was wound tightly around her throat, though he could see her hands clawing at his hold. Her black shawl fluttered on the stairs behind them.

Louisa tried to scream, tried to pull away but her assailant was strong and his grasp on her throat was merciless. She fought unconsciousness even as she fought to be free. The stone steps cut into her ankles as she was pulled along their rough edges. Just as violently, she was free and rolling down the rest of the steps. There was someone shrieking, and the close regard of several dozen people who crowded around her when she came to rest at the edge of the street.

"Back away," she heard a man's voice demand. "Let her breathe."

"Louisa," Devon said her name insistently until she opened her eyes and looked at him.

His face was pale and shadowed at once in the street lamp's light. "Devon, I—"

"Don't try to talk," he admonished. "I am going to try and discern if there is anything broken through this piece of armor you are wearing. If I hurt you, tell me."

"Lord Stanton!" Lady Townsend reprimanded as she came down to the scene.

"He is just checking for injuries, Clarisse," Lord Townsend told her calmly. "Don't want to move her if she's been severely damaged, you know."

"Of course," Clarisse replied but her lips tightened as she watched His Lordship's handling of her friend. "But must he be so thorough?"

Townsend looked skyward in exasperation but did not answer. In truth, he had found the scene stimulating. Lord Stanton's fists pummeling the man into releasing the dowager was the highlight of the evening for him. It was unfortunate that they had not caught the hooligan!

Louisa winced as Devon's deft touch hit a spot on her hip.

Her quickly indrawn breath told him she was bruised and would be sore but nothing appeared to be broken. She had been fortunate. "I am going to lift you now, Louisa," he told her quietly so that only she could hear. "I shall be as careful as I can putting you into the coach. Put your arm around my neck, if you can."

Lord Townsend cleared the group that had gathered around the fallen dowager, giving Stanton room to move to his coach nearby.

"Beth," Louisa said, opening her eyes to look into Devon's clear green gaze.

"Lady Townsend will take care of escorting her home. I am going to lift you now."

Louisa bit her lip when his hand touched the sore spot on her hip but otherwise she was comfortable. His hold on her was careful and light; even though she was certain that she must weigh him down cruelly. "I can probably walk," she started to protest, putting her arm around his neck even as she spoke.

He picked her up and walked effortlessly with her, feeling the warmth and suppleness of her body even through the heavy material of her dress. Though he was concerned for her, he could not control the flash of desire that ran through him as he touched her. He did, indeed, know the truth. And he was amazed and terrified by it.

When he reached the coach, he stepped into the vehicle with her in his arms, sitting upon the seat with her clasped closely to him on his lap. His Lordship's servants, being well trained and closely attentive to his needs, closed the door on the pair and started away.

Louisa could feel Devon's heart beating against the side

of her face as she was pressed close to him. He smelled of sandalwood and fresh air and his arms were warm around her.

"I am sorry to be such a burden," she told him slowly, her throat painful. The interior of the coach was dark, intensifying her feeling of disorientation.

"You are a delightful burden, Louisa," he said quietly. "I could only wish you in this position under different circumstances."

"Lady Townsend was quite right," she replied, feeling somewhat drowsy as the coach swayed around her. "You are debauched."

She could feel the chuckle in his chest. "Lady Townsend would not know debauched if it sat beside her and took tea. Do not go to sleep, darling. You will need to be awake for the doctor."

"Oh, I do not need—"

"Oh, I believe you do. So just relax and try to endure. Or perhaps you could endeavor to enjoy it, as I am struggling to do."

She closed her eyes and smiled, liking the sound of his voice, warm and husky, near her ear.

"Are you listening to me, sweet?" he wondered, touching a finger to the side of her face.

"Mmmm."

"Answer me, Louisa, if you please. You need to stay awake until the doctor sees you." Devon had seen many head injuries in his time and he felt the cold hand of fear on his spine as he waited for her to reply.

"Yes, Devon." She sighed finally. "But I want to sleep."

"I know," he agreed. "You can sleep later. Tell me, what made you come up with this elaborate scheme for introducing your niece to society?"

"Scheme? Oh yes, the dowager. I was afraid that as myself I might not be able to help her. Of hurting Beth's chances."

"You were trying to clear the field for her?"

"Yes," she hesitated. "Michael is gone and I promised my father I would care for the estate. If I marry, I shall lose it."

"And you have put a great deal of work into the estate to let Andrew lose it in a game of chance?"

"Yes. And it is my home, Devon. I shall not marry. I have everything I need."

"Really?" he wondered. "You have an estate, Louisa. A great, huge house and servants, horses, and tenants. What about you? Do you require nothing more? No love. No one to share your dreams? No one to hold you in the night when you awaken?"

Louisa had no answer to those questions. She had asked them herself many times but his voice made her want to weep.

The coach stopped and the driver jumped down to open the door for his Lordship to alight.

"Is there a problem, my lord?" Fleet inquired.

"Yes. Her Grace is in need of a doctor, quickly. She has been attacked and needs attention at once." Devon climbed the stairs with her in his arms, reluctant to lay her in the huge old bed. She felt right in his arms, as right as he had recalled from that day at Osbourne.

"Thank you, Devon," she whispered.

There was a trickle of blood at the side of her mouth. He dabbed at it after he wet his handkerchief at the side table. He sat beside her on the bed. "I seem to be adept at picking you up off the ground, Louisa," he observed, carefully cleaning the trace of blood.

"Yes." She tried to keep still.

"This face paint is disgusting," he told her. "I hope your niece is worth it."

Her eyes grew fierce on his. "She is worth that and more, my lord. My brother Michael would have seen to it had he lived, but Beth's mother—"

"I did not mean to distress you," he said softly. "I realize how important this is to you."

"Thank you. And thank you for your assistance at the theatre. I cannot imagine why that man chose to attack me."

"Can't you? You probably looked an easy target."

"I suppose." She sighed, every bone in her body feeling as though she had been thrown from a horse.

The doctor chose that moment to appear, with Beth at his side. He ushered Devon from the room. Beth invited Devon to the study, offering him something to drink. Fleet anticipated her request, bringing brandy and sherry in to them.

"I want to thank you for what you did for my great-aunt," Beth started when Fleet had left them, the door standing open with a footman yawning outside of it.

"It was my pleasure, Miss Montgomery," he acknowledged. "It is unfortunate that the man got away. Did the authorities arrive after we had left?"

"Yes, but they seemed to have no clues. They intimated that this sort of thing happens and that they would probably never know who attacked Aunt Louisa."

Devon frowned, considering the attack. "It is surprising to me that he did not simply steal her purse. Why drag her through the crowd?"

"She is—er—older," Beth added after a hefty swallow of her wine. "Perhaps—"

"I know, Miss Montgomery, that your aunt is not that old. However, the thief could not know that since the two of you have been so very clever as to have fooled everyone else."

He smiled at her and she swallowed wrongly, choking and coughing until he patted her on the back. "But perhaps you are right. He might have been thinking about her jewels."

The doctor joined them shortly, shaking His Lordship's hand. "She will be fine. There was nothing serious done to her that a few days' rest will not cure. She is young enough and strong enough to endure, though she will probably be a bit nervy for a while."

"Thank you, Doctor."

Devon gave Beth a speaking glance as he accompanied the doctor to the door. It was plain to see that she was terrified that the man would tell everyone what he had just told them.

"Go to your aunt," he whispered confidingly. "I shall handle the good doctor."

Beth ran up to Louisa's room. She stood beside her bed, looking at her aunt's pale face in the lamplight. Betty had come in and made her comfortable, cleaning the paint from Louisa's face and taking the pins from her elaborate coiffure.

Jane Winslow sat to one side, weeping quietly as though the woman on the bed was not long for the world.

Louisa opened her eyes slowly. She looked at her niece's troubled countenance and then frowned over Jane's continued crying. "I am all right, Beth. Do not fret. I will be right as rain by tomorrow. It was no more than a bad fall."

"I was so scared, Aunt Louisa. What if I lost you? You are so good. What if he had killed you?"

"Now, Miss Beth." Betty bustled around the room, frowning when she heard the teary voice, nudging Louisa's companion.

"I am sorry. I do not mean to be a watering pot." Beth sniffed.

Louisa and Betty exchanged glances. "Now then, miss," Betty comforted Beth. "Let me take you to your room. It will all be better in the morning. Your aunt needs her rest now."

Louisa sighed as Betty took Beth away, full-scale tears reddening her pretty face. She pushed herself up on the pillow and groaned. She was sore but no more so than any of the few times Nostradamus had thrown her. Her lip was going to be slightly swollen where she had bit it and her throat was scratchy.

Her nerves were frayed and the sound of Jane's crying was irritating. "Jane, please, dear!"

"I am so sorry." Mrs. Winslow wept.

"I understand, dear." Louisa smiled at her. "Please do not trouble yourself on my account. I shall be fine."

"I shall be just down the hall if you need me." She sniffed prodigiously, telling herself that she had known from the beginning that there would be trouble.

"Ah!" His Lordship remarked coming back into the room. "It is the Duchess of Osbourne, I believe. How wonderful to see you again!"

Louisa tried to smile and winced, the corner of her mouth sensitive. "You are not only debauched, my lord, but sadly lacking in sensibilities."

He bowed low to her, his eyes glowing in the light. "One can only hope, Your Grace. I thought you would be asleep by now with a large dose of the good doctor's laudanum in you."

She made a face. "I shall not drink such vile stuff. I believe I can become well without that poison in me."

"It might be best for later," he rejoined, his gaze on her too bright eyes and flushed countenance. He glanced around the room quickly for any other lingering relations but the room appeared to be empty.

"No thank you, my lord."

He shrugged. "Very well. What about some sherry?"

"That would be very welcome," she agreed. "There is some on the sideboard there, if you would not mind."

"Not at all. I shall give this to your maid," he said, taking the glass of laudanum from her bedside table.

She watched him pour the sherry, his broad back to her. The light was golden in his hair. Even as she wondered if she would be able to move the next morning, she felt her body react to the mere sight of him. She groaned softly, hating to admit her own need of him.

He came back to her, handing her the glass, watching her drink. "Are you in pain, Louisa?"

She closed her eyes briefly on that too attractive face. How could she tell him that a painful wanting had lodged within her and threatened to eclipse her other injuries? "I am fine, thank you." Her reply was stiff on lips that wanted to say so many other things.

"You will be glad to hear that I have spoken with the doctor and your masquerade is safe," he told her.

She had not considered that aspect. "Thank you, my lord. I appreciate your aid. Again."

"Then I would ask you to call me Devon. Again."

She looked down at the bedclothes and put her empty glass on the table beside her. "You do know all the truth, don't you? I know you must think me foolish."

"I do not think you foolish." He smiled gently. "Adorable. Intriguing. A bit too willing to rush in—"

"Please." She held up her hand to stop him, noting as she did that her arm felt incredibly heavy. "Do not go on."

"Oh, you have heard all this before? I have bored you to tears, no doubt."

"No, I—" She looked up at him, feeling very warm and sleepy suddenly. Her voice was slightly slurred. "Devon, you—"

"Yes. I do apologize, sweet. But you are tense. You would never have been able to sleep. Tomorrow, I shall visit so that you may call me vile names. Until then." He kissed her softly and pulled up the coverlet. "Sleep well."

She did not feel the touch of his lips on her brow or see him leave. The bed was soft and warm around her and the deepness of her dreams called irresistibly for the night.

Andrew hailed Lord Stanton on the street the following morning, as he was about to jump up on the high seat of his curricle. "You are about rather early!"

"I could say the same of you, Andrew. What could bring you out at this ungodly hour?" Devon took the reins from his groom and glanced out at the traffic in the street.

"I am to ride with Miss Montgomery this morning. Say, could you drop me that way, if you are going?"

"Climb up," Stanton replied, curious that Louisa would allow such a thing to happen. "But sit still, for goodness sake." This as Andrew squirmed in his place beside him. The curricle started forward. The horses were fresh, pacing themselves impatiently at Devon's expert hand. Pedestrians made way for the rigs that sped by. A street accident could mean dismemberment and drivers were not held to blame.

"I had to give up my rig," Andrew told him at last.

The Dowager Duchess   141

"Well, I mean, I lost it in a game. Aunt Louisa raised my allowance but not decently enough to give me any leeway."

"Perhaps you play too deeply," Devon remarked, not really interested in Andrew's plight.

Andrew winked conspiratorially. "It shall not matter for much longer. It is only a matter of time."

"Does the dowager know that you are riding with her niece this morning?" Devon decided to broach the matter outright.

"Well." Andrew looked away from the older man. "We, that is, Beth and I, thought it would be best—"

"If you sneaked about behind the dowager's back and risked ruining the young lady's reputation? You show your concern for the lady, as well as your game." Devon's quick retort was loaded with insult. The young man had much to learn. But not from him. He made it a strict policy not to meddle.

Andrew's cheery countenance sagged prodigiously. "I had not stopped to consider."

"Perhaps it would be wise to do so before damage is done," Devon advised, despite his better judgment. "After all, if you love the girl—"

"Love?" Andrew stopped to think upon his words.

"You will want her to be your Duchess, someday," Devon finished; glad the young man was not his responsibility. How Louisa could have taken on her niece's life was more than he could fathom. It looked to be tortuous as any war.

"Love?" Andrew was dumbfounded.

"It is obviously too early for your brain to be working properly," Devon suggested wryly, glancing at Andrew's face. He pulled the horses to a halt in front of the dowager's townhouse, acknowledging Fleet's nod as the butler sent a young messenger off on an errand.

"I think I must consider your words, Lord Stanton," Andrew declared, glancing nervously at the open door leading into the house. "Please convey my regrets to Miss Montgomery, if you should see her."

Devon watched Andrew walk briskly away from the townhouse. He heard Fleet greet Miss Montgomery and lowered himself to the street, leaving the curricle to his tiger.

"Miss Montgomery." Devon took her arm as she stood, looking down the street hopefully. "I believe I must have a word with you." Meddling was becoming a habit, he considered, and one he would give up as soon as he had done his last part for God and Country.

"But I—"

"He is not coming this morning, young lady, but you and I *will* talk. Now, if you please." Devon escorted her into the house, Beth looking shamefaced and uneasy. His words were not kind but to the point.

Beth wrung her hands and glanced up at him. "But Aunt Louisa would not allow me to ride with Andrew. If she knew that I felt anything at all for him—"

"Which you do," Devon remarked, somewhat needlessly as it was plainly written on her glowing young face.

"Well, I know that Aunt Louisa says that he is a gambler and a wastrel but I find his company quite . . . congenial."

Devon silently reviewed Andrew's untimely sprint down the street when he had heard the word "love." Beth's pretty, doll-like features were animated and very lovely but perhaps Andrew merely meant to dally with the girl. It might be in all their best interests if he told Louisa what was going on behind her back. Devon certainly did not want whatever happened between the two young people to come between them.

"You will not tell Aunt Louisa, will you, Lord Stanton?" she asked, as though reading his mind.

Devon sighed. It was obvious that she was prepared to plead with him. He was not a saint. "If you give me your word that you will not meet with him alone again. Your aunt has gone to a great deal of trouble to give you this Season. It seems fair somehow that you do not cause a scandal."

"All right." She nodded, starting to walk towards him. "You have my word." She offered him her hand.

"How is your aunt this morning?" Stanton asked, taking her small hand and releasing it quickly. He attempted to extricate himself from the uneasy role he had assumed as guardian of this young woman's reputation. A role many of his friends would find amusing, if they knew.

"She is well, if a trifle irritable." She sighed and walked to the fireplace looking at the portrait of Great-Aunt Louisa. "I wish I had never begged her to help me. All of this has been so hard for her."

"I am certain she has done it because she cares for you so very much," Devon answered calmly, although privately he had to agree. His life would be a deal less complicated if Louisa were not wearing face paint and pretending to be twenty years older than she really was. As for Louisa herself, she had been a different person at Osbourne. The tension she felt was palpable when he was with her now. Her smile was shadowed by fear.

Beth turned back to him, the ghost of a smile on her pretty face. "It is the most incredibly brave thing I have ever seen anyone do."

"Brave?" He queried. "Foolish. Ill advised, perhaps. You

do realize what will happen to her if she is found out? What will happen to you?"

She stared at him, horror struck for an instant then her face crumpled and she began to sob. "And it will be all my fault! I shall never forgive myself."

Devon went to her side, putting an arm around her shoulder. "Do not fret, Miss Montgomery. I shall do all I can not to allow that to happen, as I am certain you will."

"Well!" Mrs. Winslow humphed, entering the morning room, seeing His Lordship trying to comfort the poor girl.

Beth moved away from Lord Stanton's side, smoothing back her hair with a shaky hand. "Uh—is Aunt Louisa well enough to receive visitors?"

Jane Winslow glared at Lord Stanton as he stood, flicking an imaginary speck of lint from his faultless white shirt. "She is probably well enough to receive the Prince himself!" She humphed again. "But I wouldn't show him up to her room, the mood she's in. I wouldn't take my worst enemy up there."

Beth appeared taken aback. "Aunt Louisa has always been kind to me."

"I would not go up there, Elsbeth, if I were you. Not if you want to keep that opinion of her. She has asked me to leave several times. She is not herself."

"I would like to see her anyway," Devon volunteered, hearing Beth's quick sigh of relief.

Mrs. Winslow shrugged. "I won't try to stop you, my lord. But I should warn you that the little upstairs maid just went down to the kitchen in tears."

Devon bowed quickly to her. "As I am not an upstairs maid, perhaps I can storm the dragon's lair."

"Be careful, Lord Stanton," Beth advised.

He started up the stairs, taking a footman aside for a

quick word first. He sent the young man to the kitchen. Devon knocked on the bedroom door. Beth and Mrs. Winslow stared fearfully at his back as he opened the door and started into the room.

"I do not want a cup of chocolate, Betty," Louisa told him from her place at the window, her bedclothes trailing out beside her.

Devon did not speak for a moment, his eyes resting thoughtfully on the sight of her. Sunlight streamed through the silk of her hair, illuminating the fineness of her nightclothes so that they shadowed her slender body. "Good morning, Your Grace," he spoke at last, closing the door behind him and leaning against it. "I have come for the vile curses you were not able to utter last evening."

She barely turned to acknowledge him. "My head is pounding. I ache all over and that hideous stuff you tricked me into drinking last night has made my stomach wretched."

"You forgot your poor throat," he enjoined, seating himself on a nearby footstool. "It must hurt a great deal since you sound like a rusty gate."

Her eyes widened on him, taking in his high boots and tan jacket. He looked horribly healthy to her wretched gaze. "Go away."

A brief knock on the door brought him to his feet. He took a tray with one tall glass upon it from the footman who glanced warily into the room then disappeared. Devon closed the door and brought the glass into the room. "Drink this. It will make you feel more the thing."

Louisa looked at it as though it were a glass of poison. "I shall not drink that! After what you did last night, I shall never trust you again."

"It is nothing devious; only a little honey, some lime,

and a drop of brandy. It will help." He brought the glass to her.

She looked at it then looked up at him. "I do not want it. Nor shall I drink it."

He smiled and held the glass out to her. "Then I shall be forced to go directly to Silence Jersey and tell her the truth about her good friend, the Dowager Duchess of Roth."

"You would not!" she demanded, sitting up straighter in the window seat. Her eyes blazed blue fire.

His gaze was fastened closely on hers as he put the glass into her hand. "Are you willing to take that gamble, Madame?"

She was weak. That had to be it, she considered angrily. Just as she could not sustain Ben Robert's squint, she could not hold Devon's intent stare. "All right." She took the glass and drank it down, ignoring his smile of satisfaction. "There. You can leave now, my lord." The drink was cool and soothing to her throat. Her stomach did seem to settle almost as soon as she drank it.

"Admit it," he baited her gently, "you do feel better."

She raised her dark blue eyes to his face. "Would you have told Lady Jersey about the charade?" She had to know.

"Never," he replied sincerely. "Not if she tortured me."

Louisa smiled slightly, admitting to herself that she did indeed feel better after the concoction he'd coerced her into drinking. It was strange to have this man hovering solicitously over her. Somehow she would not have guessed it of him.

"Now, something light to break your fast, I think," he expressed heartily, standing up straight.

"Nothing for me."

"Louisa, you must eat something to recover your strength," he protested.

"Who let you into the house?" she asked, smiling ruefully. "It is not quite decent to be badgered about in one's own home this way. Have you no one else to bully?"

"Alas, no. And I find myself in quite a bullying mood, Your Grace." He shrugged, taking her hand in his own, helping her to her feet. "I must be diligent about your health."

"How kind of you to take such effort with me, my lord, when I am certain there are other more important things to occupy your valuable time." She faced him squarely but did not take her hand from his.

"If you do not feel like going down for something, I shall have something sent up," he obliged her, the familiar warmth creeping into his body when he touched her.

"I shall go down. I believe the exertion will be good for me." She caught his river green gaze observing her. "If that meets with your approval, my lord?"

"Indeed, Your Grace." He bowed slightly. "Although you seem in top form to me." His gaze, accompanied by a lecherous smile, swept over her near transparent garment, from the dainty foot that peeped out from beneath the hem of her nightdress, to the top of her shining blond hair.

Chapter Nine

Louisa colored slightly and swept a hand across her bosom in a protective gesture. "You have me at a disadvantage." She stepped back as he stepped closer. "Surely you would not want me to feel pressed into anything unseemly. No gentleman—"

He nodded briefly, catching and holding her eyes, feeling the rise and fall of her steadily increasing breaths as though they were his own. Her hand still trapped in his, he took the other away from her chest, his knuckles barely grazing her breast. "No gentleman, perhaps, Louisa, love, but a man of flesh and blood." He kissed each of her soft white hands then placed them on his shoulders.

She glanced behind her, wanting to step back once more but her legs were against the bedside.

"That may be the worst of two evils, my sweet," he advised her in a husky voice, his breath touching her cheek before his lips touched her. "My kiss and caress as we stand here. Or perhaps something more as we lie upon your bed."

"That is not much of a choice, Devon," she told him breathlessly, her eyes held hopelessly by the form and exquisite touch of his lips. She watched his head lower slowly, trapped by his nearness. Something melted inside of her as she felt his lips move deftly on her throat.

"It is the only one you are likely to have at the moment, my darling," he told her gently, while his hands gathered her closer to him. "I thought I had lost you."

It was too late, she realized, to make any choice. His mouth was already on her own, a sweet shaft of ecstasy sharp enough to be painful cutting through her. She shivered and pressed closer, forgetting that she was in her thin night rail with virtually nothing between her body and his touch.

He supported her body easily with his own, enfolding her lovingly against him so that she must feel the hard ache within him. Devon felt a tiny thrill run through her and deepened their kiss. The world had swallowed them both, hiding them in a soft, warm cocoon.

Then he heard a knock on the door, timid at first then more daring until his head echoed with it. What on earth was he thinking of? He looked down at Louisa's well-kissed lips and closed eyes, wanting to take her back in his arms even as the knocking insisted again.

"Your Grace," Betty's voice came from the other side of the door. "The doctor is here to see you. And a Bow Street Runner."

"What shall I do?" Louisa whispered at a loss, gazing up at Devon, panic stricken.

"Never fear," he replied, once again finding himself in an unusual role. "Get into bed. Quickly, love."

"Devon?" she whispered in doubt.

"Trust me." He kissed her lightly and held back the cover.

"How many ladies have fallen prey to that blandishment?" she grumbled, following his lead nonetheless.

He waited until she was in the bed, the coverlet drawn up to her chin. "Close your eyes. You are asleep."

Louisa did as he bid her, her heart pounding.

"Her Grace is still abed," Devon told Betty as he opened the door.

Betty sniffed, glancing into the room beyond him. "She was awake before."

"Perhaps she just needed a bit more rest. If you would wake her and get her ready for the doctor, I shall show him up and then deal with the Runner."

Betty looked at him, not quite trusting him but also not daring to call him a liar. "I'll do what I can, Your Lordship but if she's like she was before—"

"Everyone, I am certain, will understand, if after her ordeal, she is slightly out of countenance with the world today. Do what you are able."

With Betty's back to her, Louisa caught Devon's quick smile, then sighed as he closed the door behind him and left the room.

The doctor pronounced her fit and able to leave her bed, even encouraging her to go downstairs. "I am not one of those physicians that holds with the belief that a woman should be idle. Fresh air, walking, riding. All of these are beneficial."

"Thank you, Doctor," Louisa replied meekly. "I shall attend you."

He nodded sternly then left her there, an odor of medicine wafting through the room after his departure.

"Help me to dress, Betty," Louisa told the maid as she slowly left her bed. "I feel I should go downstairs."

"Lord Stanton is dealing with the Runner downstairs, Your Grace. Perhaps you should wait. It might be most unpleasant."

"It might be more unpleasant if I do not appear as the dowager and they come up to find another woman in her stead." She swung her legs over the edge of the bed. She was a little dizzy but not certain if it was related to the accident or Devon's embrace! "Lord Stanton dealt with the doctor. I do not know if he can ask a Bow Street Runner to ignore my charade as well."

Betty sighed but did not argue. They made up her face and hair and pulled out a voluminous brocade dressing gown that would do nicely for the dowager to be resting in after her ordeal.

"If you will assist me, Betty," Louisa said, using the deeper, huskier voice that marked her as the dowager.

Betty came and took her arm, starting down the stairs even as Lord Stanton was on his way back up.

"Your Grace." He nodded, hating to see Louisa in the makeup again yet glad that she was wise enough to know that it would be required. The Bow Street Runner would not be as easy to fob off. "I can send the Runner away for today, if you wish but he insists that he will have to talk with you about the experience at some point."

Louisa inclined her head slightly. "I am ready to receive him, Lord Stanton. Thank you for your help."

"Of course. May I assist you?" He took her arm from

Betty, walking closely alongside her down the stairs and the hallway to the study where Fleet had put the inquisitor. "Are you up to this, Louisa?" he asked quietly as they neared the room. A footman waited her decision, his white-gloved hand on the brass door handle.

"I am quite certain." She patted Devon's hand absently. "It is best to get this unpleasantness out of the way, don't you think?"

Devon had to admire her sangfroid as she sailed into the parlor under her own steam, head high. Her eyes were as brilliantly blue as sapphires.

The Bow Street Runner and his assistant were polite, deferential, and totally inadequate to deal with the Duchess. Their questions were brief and careful. When handling the Aristocracy, one could never be careless. A velvet hand was needed, never hinting at a stronger mettle. A word to one's superiors and one could be on the street.

Louisa was slightly arrogant, a bit angry. Her black cane tapped the floor more than once to punctuate her statement. Devon watched in wonder. She should have been born to the stage. Once or twice, he had to hide a smile beneath a careful hand. The authorities were quite out of their league. Fleet offered refreshments but the two men declined and left soon after.

The chances were that they would never know who had attacked the Duchess but thankfully she was not seriously hurt. In crowds of any sort there was always the opportunity for a rowdy troublemaker to make his mark. Especially with an older woman as a target. That, it appeared, was their verdict.

Louisa waxed on a little about there being no respect anymore. Didn't anyone know their place as they had when she was a young woman? Was no one safe on the streets anymore? The performance was exhausting and a collective sigh went up from the co-conspirators when the Runner had gone.

Beth glanced at her aunt who looked up at Lord Stanton.

"I believe there is breakfast in the morning room, is that not correct, Fleet?" Devon asked cheerfully.

"Indeed, my lord," the butler responded with a slight bow from his stiff, black-clad form.

"I ate some time ago but I find myself in need of further sustenance. May I escort you ladies into the dining room?"

Each of the ladies took a proffered arm and started from the room. The hallway and foyer were deluged with flowers. Floral sprays littered every surface. The scent was overpowering.

"Everyone wishes you well, Your Grace," Devon noticed wryly. "Though they threaten to bury you in their good wishes."

"It is very kind of them," Louisa said with a smile. "However if you would look closely, I believe you would find many of these flowers are to console my niece."

Lord Stanton looked at the young beauty on his right hand side and nodded. "I can see why, Your Grace. Forgive my being honest but she is very beautiful. She reminds one of the Duchess of Osbourne. There is a distinct family resemblance, do you not think?"

Louisa would have laughed at his foolishness but her ribs hurt abominably. "Really, my lord," she replied, despite Beth's giggling. "I have always found the Duchess quite plain. Not at all a beauty like Beth."

Devon looked at the younger woman again, assessing her quite thoroughly with a practiced, wicked eye. "Perhaps you are right, Your Grace. And of course, the Duchess is so much older!"

Louisa tried not to laugh and glowered at him intensely, but his look of perfect innocence was sublime.

Beth colored fiercely and looked down to the floor, reaching out to stroke the velvet petal of a red rose as she passed. The roses were from Andrew and the broad writing on the card made her glance up at Lord Stanton, biting her lip anxiously. The message was, of course, nothing that would give them away. She was not so convinced of the man who held her arm.

Devon ignored her look of entreaty. If she were not certain where his loyalties lay, it might be just as well. Perhaps that would keep the pert miss out of trouble.

Louisa cleared her throat, refusing to continue in this irrepressible vein of humor with the servants around them. Not that they had not been exposed to far worse since her arrival. "The Duchess is but more mature, my lord. Not your sort at all, I am afraid."

Lord Stanton escorted her to her place at the table and whispered near her ear. "Oh, but I prefer her aunt. Whichever one you happen to be at the time."

Devon insisted on filling Louisa's plate, piling it extravagantly with food she would not be able to eat in a week. He had no sooner put it down in front of her with the admonition to clean her plate than Fleet announced that the Duchess had a visitor.

"Who is it, Fleet?" she wondered, not wanting to take any more callers that day.

The butler stepped to one side and two men in dark riding capes approached the table. Their garments were covered with dust from the road.

Lord Stanton had not moved from Louisa's side. His hand rested, protectively, on her chair.

"Your Grace?" One of the men addressed her in a gruff voice.

"Yes?" Louisa returned, wondering why Fleet had allowed such persons into the house.

"And which Duchess would that be, my darling girl?" the second man asked her in a familiar voice. He stepped forward and swept the cape from his shoulders, revealing his head and form. It was a woman dressed in breeches and a tattered shirt. Her hair was gray and swept up to the top of her head, held in a knot by what appeared to be wooden sticks.

"Aunt Louisa?" Louisa asked in disbelief.

The older woman studied her. "Truly, Louisa. Tell me that you are not impersonating me at this moment? Tell me that this is a new fashion that you brought with you from Osbourne? My reputation will be ruined!"

The room was silent.

"Coffee, Your Grace?" Fleet asked his mistress.

"I feel I shall require something far more than coffee, Fleet," she advised him. "Bring me brandy and a glass. And leave the bottle."

Every eye was fastened on her as she took her place at the head of the table. "Oh, and this is my—uh—assistant, Jerod. You can put away the sword, Jerod, my darling. Come and sit down over here with me."

Jerod was a tall, massively built man with wild black hair and eyes. His skin was deeply tanned and his features had a definite Moorish cast. He was, indeed, holding a huge, curved sword that had been hidden in the swaths of his black cloak. At her words, he bowed his head and covered it at his side. He went to the chair beside the elder Louisa, swept them all an intense look of disdain and then sat down.

Devon took the chair beside his Louisa, glad that the man hadn't meant to attack them all with that thing. He didn't know if there was a stick of furniture in the house that the sword couldn't have hacked to bits!

When they were all seated around the big table, Louisa, Dowager Duchess of Roth, looked at each one of them.

"You must be Elsbeth," she said as she identified her grand-niece. "You look a great deal like your father, and consequently, like myself. I'm sure you must be here because your mother is an idiot!"

Beth smiled ingenuously. "And it is certainly a pleasure to make your acquaintance, Great-Aunt Louisa, although I feel I know you already."

The dowager looked at Jane Winslow whose eyes were enormous and frightened as she stared at the dark-skinned man. "You, I do not know."

"Cousin Jane Winslow, Uncle Marcus' daughter," Louisa murmured, reminding her aunt.

"Ah, yes. Welcome, Jane. You look as though you just found out there was a rat in the stew! Do try not to stare at Jerod, dear. He becomes horribly offended!"

Jane Winslow blinked, then looked down at her plate.

The elder Louisa cut off one end of a small, dark cigar. Jerod leaned forward quickly to light it. Fleet set brandy, two glasses and a bottle from the cellar on the table before her.

"Jerod's religion doesn't allow him to imbibe, Fleet," she told her loyal butler. "However, he would probably enjoy some strong tea." She sent a plume of blue smoke into the air.

"Right away, Madame."

"I don't know you," she apprised Lord Stanton. "But I am certain I should like to."

"I am Stanton," he introduced himself. "And I am pleased that you are finally returned, Your Grace."

She laughed; her blue eyes so like those of her nieces, alight with the fierce joy of living. "I'll wager you are, Stanton! Correct me if I'm wrong but you seemed most protective of my goddaughter just then."

He nodded. "I assure you, I would have shielded the other ladies as well, while your friend hacked me to pieces, Your Grace."

"Jerod is formidable," she agreed. "There is something familiar about you. I am convinced that I know your father."

"That is not unlikely, Your Grace."

"Call me Louisa, Stanton! I have not been addressed as 'Your Grace' for so long that it seems foreign to me!"

"As you wish, Louisa," he murmured. "I am Devon."

Just then, Jane was seized by a violent fit of coughing. She looked around the table then rushed from the room.

"I think Mrs. Winslow does not tolerate cigar smoke well," Beth observed quietly.

The dowager snorted. "If I recall Jane, she was always a stickler for the rules. Her sensibilities are no doubt more injured than her stomach!" She turned to Louisa. "And that is why you had her here, no doubt? To lend credence to this charade?"

Louisa nodded. "She is above reproach."

Her aunt affected the same head inclination. "All right. Who is going to tell me what this is all about?"

Louisa began haltingly, glossing over a few parts, leaving out some things that were best left out. Beth took over and explained about her Mama's debts and the lecherous Viscount. She left out only her infatuation with Andrew Drayton and her plans to marry him.

The dowager, who in reality looked more like Louisa's older sister, leaned back in her chair, sipped her brandy and blew smoke up into the air. "And where do you fit in, Devon? Are you Louisa's lover?"

Louisa choked on a sip of water. She coughed and spluttered, finally putting her napkin against her mouth.

Devon grinned. The Duchess was an original. "I am the innocent, Louisa. Your niece has led me a merry chase, even going so far as offering to help me seduce her—in your guise, of course."

Louisa gaped at him. "I never did! He was trying to seduce me and I used your identity to put him in his place."

Aunt Louisa, Great-Aunt Louisa, laughed out loud. "From where I am sitting, my darling, he appears to be the more believable of the two of you! Do go and change into whatever you look like when you are at Osbourne. I don't think the world is ready for two of me!"

"When did you get back?" Louisa wondered. "Why are you dressed this way?"

Great-Aunt Louisa reached into a pocket of her breeches and flipped out something that gleamed dully against the dark wood of the table. "A medallion that belonged to Phillip of Macedonia. Priceless. Why do you think that man knocked you down at the theatre, my darling? He wants that medallion!"

One by one, they looked at the jewel-encrusted circlet. It was quite heavy, clearly made of gold, although the metal was barely visible through the grime of centuries. Sapphires and rubies blinked at them in the light. Onyx and pearl created the barely recognizable silhouette of a man's face in the center.

"We dug that up a few weeks ago," the dowager explained to them. "We've had problems since then. One man in particular is obsessed with taking the medallion back to Greece. He wants to bury it again."

"How obsessed is he?" Devon wondered.

"Insanely so," she replied carefully. "He will stop at nothing."

"And this is the man who attacked me last night?" Louisa wondered.

"You were going to change, darling?" she reminded her niece. "We shall have a nice coze until you have done. Lord Stanton? Perhaps you would join me in the library."

Devon stood up quickly and held Her Grace's chair, ignoring Jerod's hard stare. "Gladly."

The dowager smiled slyly. "You live dangerously, my Lord Stanton."

"Exactly so, Your Grace."

Louisa changed her clothing quickly with Betty's help. She took off the hated face paint and cleaned her hair.

"At least you look respectable now," Betty remarked. "The duchess will be having a few words to say about all of this!"

Fortunately, they had brought a few dresses that actually belonged to Louisa. The others, she instructed Betty to give away. "I do not think Aunt Louisa will be wearing those fashions. She seems to be quite an original."

Betty nodded. "I heard from the downstairs maid that she was wearing men's breeches!"

Louisa smiled. Now that it was over, it was a relief. She could look at the whole thing and laugh. "I cannot imagine the surprise to which Aunt Louisa's friends are to be treated!"

"What about Miss Beth's Season?"

"Surely, Aunt Louisa will take over," the younger Louisa fretted. Then when she considered Aunt Louisa and her effect on the *ton*, she wasn't sure if that would help Beth at all. "I do not know as yet, Betty. First we must sort through all this madness."

Louisa joined Beth and Mrs. Winslow at the library doors. They could hear laughter and voices coming from within. Lord Stanton's deep voice was distinctive with the Duchess' sparkling laughter.

"Are we to join them?" Beth wondered a little nervously.

"So we are," Louisa replied as Fleet approached to announce them.

"I would prefer not to be in there with that heathen," Mrs. Winslow said softly.

"You could retire, dear," Louisa suggested.

"Her Grace has demanded my presence," Jane Winslow stated. "It was not a request."

The butler ignored them and pushed open the doors to the room while a young maid scurried in with tea.

"The Duchess of Osbourne, Mrs. Winslow, and Miss Elsbeth Montgomery."

Louisa entered the room, followed by the two other women. Great-Aunt Louisa was seated in one of the big chairs. Jerod was on the floor beside her. His Lordship was standing beside the fireplace.

"Fleet is so pompous! Louisa," she said to her niece. "I should appreciate it if you would pour."

Louisa nodded and took a seat on the divan behind the table on which the silver teapot and cups had been placed. Mrs. Winslow took a seat near the door and Beth sat beside Louisa.

"I have been explaining the seriousness of the situation to Lord Stanton. Being a man recently returned from the war, I believe he can help us resolve our dilemma."

"What dilemma are we facing, Great-Aunt Louisa?" Beth wondered.

"We must apprehend Spiros and give him over to the proper authorities. He is wanted all across the Continent for smuggling and extortion. Yet no one knows what he looks like. He is a deadly shadow."

Louisa poured tea into the handsome cups emblazoned with the Ducal coat of arms. "How are we to capture such a dangerous villain?" She handed a cup to Devon. His hand caressed hers and her eyes locked with his.

"Jerod and I have been laying low in one of the most detestable spots in the city," her aunt explained. "When I heard of the attack on the Dowager Duchess of Roth, I was struck with a plan!"

"A plan that is dangerous, at best," Devon enjoined.

"Nonetheless," Louisa Rothner continued. "You look quite lovely as yourself, my darling, but for one more night, I need you to play me."

"Play the dowager again?" Louisa asked, glancing at Devon as she handed Beth her tea.

"Your aunt is convinced that this man, Spiros, will have to show his hand tonight. The medallion will be given to the museum tomorrow. It would be far simpler for him to take it from you."

"Do not doubt that he has been in this house, searching for it," her aunt cautioned. She poured a liberal amount of brandy into her cup of tea then settled back in her chair. "When the library appeared to be broken into, he wanted you to know that he had been here. It was a warning. Spiros is far too good a thief to ever give himself away."

"But if the man is the vicious killer that your aunt has portrayed him, you will be risking your life out there tonight, Louisa," Devon warned. "The operation is sound and has worked thousands of times but not without serious risk."

Louisa sipped her tea and glanced around the room. She wished she could speak with Devon alone to ask his advice. Of course, she would probably do the thing anyway, just to repay her aunt for the charade she'd undertaken with her name and reputation. "So, I would be a decoy?"

"You would," her aunt agreed. "We would be watching for Spiros, without the risk that he could possibly take the medallion back. He is very likely to attack you again during the fireworks display at the park tonight. When he does, we would be there."

Louisa nodded. "Would we not be better served in a less dangerous place?"

"We would," her aunt admitted. "But Spiros will not. He would not risk capture to take back the medallion. He is not foolish, Louisa, darling. Only obsessive."

"I shall do as you ask, Aunt," Louisa said quietly. "I beg your pardon for attempting to masquerade as you."

"Your heart was in the right place, my dear child," Great-Aunt Louisa considered. "It is not news for our family to come up with unusual ways of dealing with a problem."

She outlined her plan for that evening at Vauxhall Gardens. She asked Mrs. Winslow and Beth to be present as well so that there would be extra pairs of eyes to watch for the clever knave.

"We could ask Andrew to help as well," Beth chimed in when she had finished.

Both of her aunts looked at her.

"Who is Andrew?"

"The Marquess of Osbourne," Beth related, slowly. "He is very heroic."

The two Louisas glanced at one another.

"That sounds like a situation your aunt and chaperone must deal with, dear girl," her Great-Aunt told her.

"We shall speak of this later," Louisa promised Beth.

"For now," the dowager said, standing, "I should like a bath, a meal, and my bed for the day." Jerod was on his feet and at her side at once.

"I am sleeping in your room, Aunt," Louisa informed her. "But I shall be happy to remove myself to another."

"Do not trouble yourself, darling," her aunt replied with a hand on Jerod's muscular arm. "Jerod and I have slept on the ground for months. Any bed will be a treat."

When the door had closed on the dowager and her assistant, Mrs. Winslow got to her feet abruptly. "I shall not be a party to this nonsense! I came here to help you chaperone Elsbeth and that has proved trying enough! All of this masquerading and now this! I shall not be a party to it!" So saying, the woman flounced from the room. The door closed lightly behind her.

"I believe you are promised to be part of the Countess Markland's group bound for the Tower today," Louisa reminded her niece. "We shall speak of this infatuation you hold for the Marquess later."

"Yes, Aunt Louisa," Beth answered dutifully. "But I believe you are unfairly prejudiced against him! He is not the monster you make him out to be!" Beth left the room, closing the door behind her.

"It seems we are alone," Devon observed.

Louisa sighed, not looking at him. "We should not be. I am no longer the dowager."

He knelt before her and raised her chin so that their gazes met. "No, you are not. You are a lovely, remarkable woman with eyes the color of a tropical sea and lips dusted with rose."

She searched his eyes for any sign of insincerity and not finding it, looked away. "My position has not changed, Devon."

"But mine has," he told her quietly. It was only a small movement to kiss her lips.

She shook her head but did not move away.

He kissed her again, his lips persuading her that there was much more for them to explore. He felt her hand creep up to his shoulder. Her mouth softened and parted. Her body leaned into his. He pushed gently and she leaned back against the divan. He followed her, his hands shaping and caressing her body.

"Do you love me?" he whispered as he kissed her neck and shoulders.

She moaned and gasped as his hand stroked her skin. His mouth followed his hand, tracing the line where her bodice met her soft skin, making her feel languid and floating.

"I—I—don't . . . ohhh, Devon," she groaned. "I do! I do love you!"

"I love you, too," he told her between urgent kisses. "I ache for you, Louisa. I could not bear to think of you being with another."

"Nor I," she promised. "I cannot . . . think . . . Devon . . . ohhh!"

"I am going to be quite discreet and knock on this door before I enter," the dowager announced loudly before she opened the library door.

Devon and Louisa were calmly sitting on the divan together. If Louisa's gown was a little askew and Devon's cravat, slightly wilted, the older woman wisely did not take note.

"I forgot to ask if you would be so kind as to join us tonight, Stanton," Aunt Louisa wondered.

"I shall be with your niece," he replied in a husky voice. "I do not like her being alone through this."

"As you wish," the grande dame responded, looking at them both with a critical eye. "I am going for that meal now. Pray, Louisa, darling, do not make me call Mrs. Winslow to chaperone *you*."

When they were alone, Louisa blushed like a schoolgirl.

"I beg your pardon for letting things get out of hand," Devon said, taking her hand and kissing it warmly. "The day promises to be almost as lovely as you. Come for a ride in the park with me?"

"I am not an innocent, my lord. You did not take advantage of me," she informed him tautly. Then she saw the green fire in his eyes and smiled despite herself. "But I would love to ride out with you! Anything to take my mind from this evening's events."

He handed her up into his curricle once she had fetched her bonnet and shawl. She barely wasted time on her appearance, nervous as a child about to have a sweet. "There is one thing I have wanted to ask you," she said when they had crossed the busy street and entered the park.

"I am all attention, my love."

"How did you know? For you did, didn't you?"

He smiled and glanced at her. "I knew from the day I took the dowager out for a ride."

"But how? Everyone else was fooled by the disguise."

"Indeed, it was quite clever," he admitted. "The difference is that I saw Louisa Drayton at Osbourne and I—uh—noticed rather closely her appearance. When I looked at the portrait, I noticed an incongruity."

"Incongruity?"

He nodded. "The dowager has a cleft in the top lip. You

have one, my sweet, in the bottom lip. It is almost insignificant. Except to a desperate man."

She laughed, enjoying the man and the warmth of the sun on her head. "How desperate, my lord?"

"I believed I was attracted to the dowager," he admitted. "I needed to understand rather quickly."

Louisa felt younger and more carefree than she had in years. "You were attracted to me as the dowager? Even in that awful paint and powder?"

He took her hand and kissed it. "I think my heart should know you if I were blind, Louisa."

"Devon." She sighed.

They took a less populated path that led through an area where the trees were closer together. The shade from the sun was welcome. The feeling of being alone in the world with Devon made her nervous and uneasy. It reminded her of how very much she should like to kiss him again. It was an addiction, feeling his lips on hers. She wanted it to go on and on. She found herself thinking of different ways to kiss him, different places.

Devon stopped the horses, drawing them to the side of the path. He turned to her, as though he could not resist, took her by the shoulders and drew her into his embrace. "Come with me," he invited, tickling her ear with his kisses.

"W-where?" she wondered, feeling her bonnet fall from her head.

"I'll come for you, tonight when everything is over," he planned. He kissed her passionately, their mouths fusing together, their united breaths coming faster. "Come with me," he urged her. "Promise me?"

"Y-yes," she answered. As she knew her only answer could be. "Yes."

Chapter Ten

Later, when he had left her at the dowager's townhouse, Louisa wished she had something more elaborate to wear for that night. The gowns she'd brought with her from Osbourne were quite plain. She'd had no thought of wearing anything that would not fit the dowager image.

Louisa wasn't a fool. She knew what he wanted from her. She had made up her mind that she would have it for one night. She had made her bargain with the devil and her own soul.

For one night, she would be his totally, without thinking about the future. One night would not cost her the world but it would take her through a future of lonely years without him. Then she would leave him and not look back. They would both have what they wanted and no one would be the wiser. She would go back to her farming at Osbourne. He would, doubtless, go on with his own life with any or all of the women her aunt's friends had mentioned.

It was a sad thought yet she convinced herself that it had a sublime, if tragic, quality to it. Rather like a good opera. She loved a man who loved her but they could not be together.

The Vauxhall Garden outing was planned with Colonel Parker and his niece accompanying Beth and the dowager. The crowd was overpowering. Everyone gathered together to hear the music especially composed for the affair in honor of Napoleon's final defeat. Lords and Ladies rubbed elbows with chimney sweeps and Bow Street Runners.

Louisa stood beside the Colonel in her guise as the Dowager, half listening to his incessant prattle. How the man could find enough air in his lungs to talk continuously was more than she could fathom! She glanced around herself surreptitiously, unable to really enjoy the affair because she was so worried about Spiros showing up and killing her to take the medallion. She knew her aunt and Jerod were somewhere in the crowd, along with a dozen good men that her aunt had hired.

Jerod had been a surprise. Aunt Louisa had been a shock. What would her friends say about the cigar-smoking Dowager when it was all over?

Lord Cambridge had joined their group, telling them about the extravagant pyrotechnics that were to come. Annabelle was all attention when the young gentleman spoke but Louisa noticed that Beth was distracted, her eyes following the crowd. There was no doubt in her mind that her niece had made some assignation with Andrew. It would not do, she considered, compressing her lips into a thin line of disapproval. She had not brought her niece to London to get away from one old lecher only to give her to a young lecher!

"Good evening, Your Grace; Colonel Parker. Stirring music, is it not?"

Louisa forgot when she turned to face Devon how it was that she had promised herself that she would act when she next saw him. He was standing beside her, almost touching, smiling down at her. Every thought went from her head in her pleasure at seeing him there. Immediately, she felt safer and less the target. Colonel Parker said something in return but Louisa was not certain of his words. It was at that moment that she knew that she was lost.

"I trust you are feeling well after your most unfortunate accident?" Stanton asked her directly.

"I am quite well," she replied breathlessly, certain only that he was near to her and that his eyes were laughing into hers.

He turned to speak with Lord Cambridge and the two young ladies, not moving away. She knew that just a movement of her own arm or a shift in her stance would bring them together. Of course, she would not make that movement or dare to change her footing even though twilight shadowed everything around them.

She craved his touch, spare though it would be. She had learned to her own chagrin that he was quickly becoming a necessity to her. When he was not with her, she was thinking of his last words, his final nuances. No matter how she chastised her poor brain in the early hours of the morning, there he was, and always most improperly! Kissing her, touching her until she thought she would go mad.

From her vantage point, she watched him, clever knave that he was, maneuver the group to his own direction. The Colonel was accompanying the young people to the refreshment area before he had realized that Louisa was left behind. By then the crowd had closed around them and they were being pushed in the general direction of the tables set up for the evening. Lord Stanton, gallant rogue, courteously brought the Dowager along even though they were pushed into the shadows as they walked.

"Very clever, my lord," Louisa commended as he drew her arm through his own.

"I cannot fathom your meaning, Your Grace," he replied coolly.

"Can you not? You managed to be alone with me quite ruthlessly." The shadows deepened so that she could not make out his face. "How am I to be safe?"

"And why would I do such a thing?" he demanded.

She was not certain but instinct told her that he was laughing, though his deep voice was quite steady.

"No doubt you have something evil in mind," she answered truthfully. "Perhaps it would be wise if I were to scream now."

"Better to be safe," he quoted then turned her suddenly so that she was engulfed in the darkness, the only light falling on his back.

"Devon," she opened her mouth to protest.

"Too late, I think," he observed, then kissed her.

His touch was gentle but demanding, his lips quelling any resistance, however half-hearted, that she was likely to make. It was the caress of a man who knew the woman in his arms was willing and waiting for him.

Louisa regained her equilibrium only when someone nearby laughed rather loudly. Even then, to her shame and disbelief, it was Devon that pulled back from her.

He stood very still while she attempted to correct any damage that his caress might have accomplished, glad that it was dark. "You look wonderful, darling," he assured her, tucking a stray curl into the powdered monument of her coiffure. "Even as you are, you are delicious."

"You find me attractive even in this—," she began, only to find herself at a loss for words. "Why do you do this to me?"

"I am the villain in this piece, sweet, I agree. You, the innocent, and I, the hopelessly enamored debaucher. I am certain someone should write a novel on it." He took her arm once again and began to stroll towards the tables of refreshments.

"That is not an answer," she muttered darkly.

"What you ask is not a question," he replied calmly, "but a debate men and women have had since time immemorial. Why does anyone become attracted to anyone else?"

"It is more than that," she disagreed quietly. "I have met other men."

"And they never made you feel as I do? Despite what Clarisse Townsend considers, I do not desire every woman in England. But I do seem to have a penchant for women who have dual personalities. Perhaps it is a failing."

"It is simple for you to laugh at me," she told him, embarrassed by the discussion.

"Laugh at you?" he demanded, his voice becoming lower. His head was bent close to her own. "Darling Louisa, I want to kiss every part of your sweet body. I want to wake up with you in my arms during the night. I cannot sleep for thinking of you. If I am laughing, it is a painful humor."

Louisa could not find her voice to reply.

"I have shocked you, no doubt," he said it for her, though his voice was slightly bitter.

Hers, she was certain, would have trembled, though outwardly she was composed.

"There you are, Stanton." Colonel Parker pushed his way through the crowd towards them. "A sight too many people here."

"Indeed," Lord Stanton agreed smoothly as though nothing had happened between them.

"Must be rather faint with the crush." The Colonel nodded towards Louisa. "Best get you back."

"Not before the fireworks," Annabelle protested.

"Of course not." Louisa found her voice at last. She glanced around the group. "But where is Beth?"

As the Duchess' party began to spread out through the crowd, hoping to find Beth before any damage was done, Miss Montgomery herself was promenading with Andrew along the edge of the grassy knoll.

"You have surely enjoyed your time here thus far, Miss Montgomery," Andrew remarked. "You are a success!"

Beth's eyes scanned the crowd, wondering how much time they had before she would be found out. "Being a success, sir, is not what so many think it to be."

"Oh?" He guided her carefully around a flowerbed too dark to see but the fragrance proclaimed it to be roses.

"It is all rather boring, is it not?" She sighed. "I should rather be out gaming or walking through the city at night with a group of rowdies."

Andrew was amazed and appalled. "This cannot be true. You are a well-bred young woman. How can you know of such things much less wish to try them?"

"I know of many things that I shall, alas, not be allowed to attempt. You know, sir, that my marriage is eminent."

"Someone has offered for you?" he queried, feeling unaccountable anger rise up in him. "Who is it?"

"There have been many but of course my aunt must have only the most worthy." She sighed again. "It does not matter whether I shall be bored all my life so long as he is acceptable."

"And has she found this most acceptable gentleman?" he inquired.

"I am afraid so." Beth could not see his face in the dark but his tone was satisfactorily intent. "It is only a matter of time until my imprisonment begins."

"Surely there could be someone," he paused and adjusted his throaty voice. "Someone who would not be so . . . boring."

"Perhaps," she agreed. "But he would have to be acceptable as well. I would not tell anyone but you, sir, but it seems hopeless. I hope you do not mind. I feel I can confide in you. You are different than the others."

"I—I appreciate your trust." Andrew swallowed hard. "I wish that I could do something to help you."

The moon was rising and the music was reaching its final swelling. Beth stumbled slightly as they walked down the small hill. Andrew was quick to catch her arm, pressing her close to him for an instant. The moon was silver on her hair and shone in her eyes when she looked up at him. For just a fraction of time, they were bound together by the oldest spell in the world. Their eyes feasted on each other's faces then their lips met only briefly.

"Andrew," Beth whispered, stepping back.

"I do not know what I was thinking, Miss Montgomery . . . Beth," he stammered. "I do apologize. It was the moment. I do not know what I was about—"

"Children." Lord Stanton's deep voice made them both jump. "I believe we must have a talk." Deftly, Devon found a way to introduce the couple to the crowd. Separately, of course. For those who had been paying attention, it would be difficult to know who Miss Montgomery had gone with and with whom she had come back.

It was quite a simple thing to place Beth between the Colonel and Louisa, leaving Lord Stanton to follow with Annabelle and Lord Cambridge. Nothing was said of the incident, though Louisa was seething with angry questions.

The pyrotechnics were spectacular after the concert and easily seen overhead. Everyone there declared them to be the best there had ever been. Louisa was not certain she could have told afterward what colors they were or where they had been in relation to herself.

It appeared as though Spiros was not going to make the attempt after all to recover the medallion. Louisa began to think about her assignation with Devon later that night.

Their coach was waiting in a shadowed area to the south of the Garden. Colonel Parker stated quite loudly that he would be escorting the dowager back to her townhouse.

Devon helped Beth and Annabelle into the Ducal coach. He turned to look towards Louisa in time to see the Colonel tossing a rough blanket over her head and pushing her into his coach. The driver reacted at once and the horses were off down the dark street.

Louisa felt the rasp of the suffocating material on her face. She was breathless with it. The rough shove that had precipitated her entrance to the coach had wedged her between the seats. Strong hands lifted her and set her up on the seat as the coach ran wildly through the city streets.

"Ah, my dear," the Colonel said, removing the cloth from her head and face. "I apologize for my ungentle treatment of you."

"You!" she accused, trying to maintain her seat on the coach. "What are you doing?"

"Alas, I would like this to be a romantic assignation,

Your Grace, but the truth is that I have come for the medallion. As you knew I would." He rubbed a dirty cloth over his face and stripped a white wig from his head. "We meet again, Duchess! The years have been kind to you!"

"Spiros!"

"Indeed! You knew I was after you and the medallion. You are not so empty headed as you seem."

"But the real Colonel Parker—"

"—is at home with a mighty headache, no doubt. Do not worry. He will recover. Perhaps he will not speak so much, hmm?"

"I do not have the medallion," she told him bluntly.

"Then you know where it is hidden. Take me there."

Louisa looked at the man with the wild black hair and the black eyes. He looked capable of anything. She was terrified but she knew she must play for time. Someone would have noticed that she was abducted. Devon was not that far away.

"How do I know you won't kill me if I take you to it?"

Spiros smiled evilly. "You do not. And I give you no assurances. But you have already led me a chase. I leave England tonight. With the medallion. Or your head. It is your choice."

She smiled though her heart felt like a cold stone in her chest. The horses were running madly through the night. They could be anywhere. She had to think of some place to tell him where the medallion was hidden. It must be a place they would consider looking for her.

"You have been through my house?"

"Of course. The medallion is not there." He pulled an ugly knife from his boot. "Take me to it, Duchess. Do not play games with me."

The coach swayed dangerously and Spiros was flung

against the door. Louisa was heaved on the floor like so much baggage.

"What is going on out there?" he demanded angrily.

Louisa tried to think of any place, in London or out. She couldn't even recall the name of her own estate at that moment! You have to think, she prodded her mind, as she pushed herself back up on the seat. Where should you take him? It appeared to be a meaningless question, however, as the coach slowed and stopped in the street.

Spiros yelled something in Greek out the window to the driver. The driver mumbled something unintelligible back to him. Spiros cursed and threw open the door.

Lord Stanton had him the minute his boots hit the wet street. He knocked the man to the ground then moved away quickly as Spiros came after him with his knife. Long nights in the seamy lanes of London and Paris stood His Lordship well. He was never quite where Spiros thrust his dirty knife, yet he managed with each thrust to hit his opponent squarely in a vital body organ.

Spiros screamed, enraged, and ran towards Devon with the knife high in the air. Devon turned on his heel. Spiros rushed by but not before His Lordship had managed a well-placed kick that sent his opponent, face down, to the ground. Spiros stayed where he had fallen. Devon bent over him carefully and found the blade, buried to the hilt in the other man's chest.

Louisa was out of the coach and in his arms before he could think or react to what had happened. She covered his face in kisses and quickly looked him over to be certain that he was not injured. Then she wept. "How did you find me?"

"I jumped on the back of the coach as he was making

off with you. It was just a matter of us getting the driver to stop."

"Us?" she asked, looking around them on the dark street.

Someone jumped down from the coachman's seat and bowed low before her. "Your Grace." It was Andrew!

"Andrew jumped on the coach a moment after I, Your Grace," Devon explained. "He made his way to the coachman's seat and threw off the blackguard so that he could take his place and stop the coach. The rest, I believe you know."

"You are very brave," Louisa commended, not sure if she looked or sounded like the dowager anymore, not certain that she cared. It was over. She would never be the Dowager Duchess of Roth again.

"Thank you, Your Grace," Andrew accepted her praise modestly. "It was something any gentleman would have done. But perhaps you could put in a word with Miss Montgomery's aunt?"

"I shall, indeed," Louisa promised quietly. "Now, it is late and I require rest after such a harrowing experience. I would thank you both for seeing me home."

The Colonel's coach went back down the streets more somberly. At the townhouse, Louisa was greeted with hugs and tears from Beth and Annabelle. The real Colonel Parker had managed to free himself and call the Runners. Andrew and Devon told them their story while Louisa slipped upstairs.

Between the fall on the theatre steps and her thwarted kidnapping that evening, she was more than a little sore and bruised. She let Betty help her with her makeup and instructed her to get rid of the dowager's last dress. Betty left her alone in a hot bath, contemplating her future. Louisa had not been private with Devon from the moment she found that he had saved her. Would he still want her to meet him that night?

And Andrew had been there to save her! What was she to make of that? Her world was askew! Perhaps he was the hero that Beth had proclaimed him.

There was a knock at the door and Aunt Louisa popped her head around. "I should like to speak with you, Louisa, darling."

Louisa covered herself modestly with a cloth and bade her aunt enter.

"You look not much the worse for wear," her aunt told her, assessing her face quickly.

"It was terrible," Louisa told her. "I could not think. I felt like a frightened rabbit."

Aunt Louisa shrugged her slim shoulders. "You kept your wits about you enough that Spiros didn't kill you. That is all that matters. Now, the other!"

"Other?" Louisa asked, feeling her bath water grow tepid.

"This business with you and Devon." Her aunt came straightaway to the point.

"Devon?" she asked in a small voice.

"Don't pretend you are ignorant of his bribing a footman to tell you that he will await you tonight at midnight outside the townhouse! What am I to make of this, Louisa? Are you so innocent that you do not know what this man is about?"

Louisa looked down at the cloth that covered her chest. Then she looked up at her aunt. "I am two and twenty, Aunt Louisa. I have run an estate and I am responsible for many lives. And for the first time in my life, I am in love. I wish we could have more than just this one night but it is all there is for us. I plan to cherish it."

The elder Louisa laughed and lit up a cigar. "You are indeed my godchild! The first footman had this note for you." She handed Louisa the paper. "Tomorrow, the museum takes the medallion and I must decide to stay in London or to return to Greece with Jerod for he goes with or without me. He is not one who can live tamely in the city, you see. Enjoy your night, child. Sometimes, it is all we have."

Louisa watched her aunt leave then climbed from the cooled tub. She rubbed herself dry but could not seem to get warm. *Devon will warm me.* She smiled at the thought and dressed quickly. She looked at the note again.

"My driver and carriage will be at your doorstep at midnight. Come to me if you can, Devon."

Betty helped her pull on the gown of rich blue silk with the pearl fasteners. Her father had always said that blue made her eyes seem deep. The maid dressed her hair with loose curls cascading down her shoulders and placed a sprig of blue cornflowers in her hair.

"You look like a young girl again," Betty told her wistfully.

Louisa looked at her maid in the mirror. "What? No lecture?"

Betty sniffed. "You have a right to be happy. I'll say no more."

Louisa pulled on her heavy cloak and gave Betty a hug. "Thank you. I will be happy. At least for tonight."

If she had thought it would be difficult to whisper down the long stairway in the quiet house, she was wrong. Fleet was nowhere in sight. Perhaps it was a matter that her aunt had attended to for her.

Surprisingly, she felt light of heart and foot. If she expected to feel guilty, she did not. She felt as though she had waited for Devon her whole life. It was his love that she had been cheated of when her mother had died and she had run back to Osbourne. Battered and bruised, she went to him. She would have gone if she'd had to crawl.

The footman helped her into the closed coach without a word. The streets were very dark and quiet. From the distance came the sound of the Watch. The footman closed the door and Louisa drew the shade on the window. Alone with her thoughts and her anticipation, she sank back against the comfortable squabs and waited for the journey to end.

It was over much faster than she had allowed. Or at least it seemed that way to her. The door was opened and the stairs let down. Louisa had promised herself that she would not look around herself. She would not condemn or try to discover where Devon had thought to bring her. She had no doubt that it would not be to his home.

But this! She stood on the street for a moment, taking it in. It was dark, but even so, she could not miss where she found herself.

"Louisa!" Devon came to her side, taking her hand. He kissed her cheek. "You are as beautiful as the night."

Louisa looked up at him. "What are you about, Devon? I thought, I *assumed*—"

He whisked her away from the coach. "I know what you assumed, my love. But this is the sad reality. You see before you a man; humbled by a woman who cannot make up her mind which Duchess she wants to be. So, I have decided, with her consent, to make her my Lady and strive each day to clear her confusion."

Louisa looked up at the face of the huge, centuries-old church. "How is this possible?"

"I have obtained a special license and enlisted the aid of

a reputable minister. When I told him my story, he took pity on me and agreed to this rather unusual wedding service."

Louisa smiled. "Are you sure, my lord? I am likely to be confused about which Lady I am as well."

Devon bent his head and kissed her lips while the stars spun around her and the world tilted. "I vow that I shall be relentless in reminding you that you belong to me and I to you, my love. I love you. Last night, when Spiros took you away, was closer to death than anything that happened to me during the War. I would not want to live without you."

"Then I suppose I shall have to agree," she told him with a sigh. "I only hope you are prepared for me to grub around on your estate until it meets my expectations."

"Grub away. I shall grub with you. And our children."

Louisa blushed and took his hand. "I love you, Devon. I think I should like to be your bride."

It was the following afternoon when Louisa returned to the townhouse. With Stanton at her side, she descended from the curricle. He kissed her quickly then they turned to go inside.

"Louisa!" Aunt Louisa greeted her at the door. "What have you done?"

"Aunt?"

"Spending a night of pleasure with a man is one thing but you must be discreet! Coming back in the middle of the day! Kissing your paramour in the street! Your reputation will be in shreds! No decent hostess will have you, or Beth for that matter! What are you thinking?"

"And you, Devon!" She turned to His Lordship. "I cannot believe you care so little for Louisa's reputation that you would allow her to besmirch herself this way!"

"I care so much for her reputation, in fact, Your Grace, that I married her early this morning." He held up both their ringed hands.

Aunt Louisa frowned. "Oh my. I need a brandy. And a cigar. Fleet!"

"Aunt Louisa! Aunt Louisa!" Beth came running breathlessly to the front door.

"Are we so lacking in propriety that we must air our private matters in the street?" Aunt Louisa asked. "Fleet! Brandy and a cigar!"

"Your pardon, Aunt Louisa. Aunt Louisa. My Lord. But my father! I have had word from my father!"

"Michael?" Louisa asked tearfully.

"He is alive. Injured but coming home. He is alive!"

Beth and Louisa both hugged Devon and each other.

The dowager shook her head. "It seems we must have a celebration! Fleet! Two bottles of brandy and a box of cigars, if you please!"

Devon looked at Louisa. "Your aunt is truly an original."

Louisa sighed and smiled. "I feel certain you told me the same thing earlier this morning, my lord."

Devon smiled devilishly. "So I did, Lady Stanton. And I am likely to do so again."

"Soon, I hope?" she whispered as Jerod and Fleet joined them.

"Very soon," he promised.

repair 3-04 dog chewed corner